PROTEST!

BY
STEVE FINBOW
MELISSA MANN
JOSEPH RIDGWELL

© 2009 Copyright remains with Steve Finbow, Melissa Mann and Joseph Ridgwell.

All rights reserved; no part of this publication may be reproduced in any way without the written consent of:

Beat the Dust Press
90 Cannock Court
3 Hawker Place
Walthamstow
LONDON
E17 4GD

Protest! cover designs, editing and typesetting by Steve Finbow, Melissa Mann, Joseph Ridgwell and Chandler Book Design.

Cover images used without permission. Please don't bother suing us cos we ain't got the dosh. Author mugshots by Vince Wade.

ISBN: 978-0-9563618-0-6

Beat the Dust Press UK 2009
www.beatthedust.com/press.asp

Printed in Great Britain by the MPG Books Group, Bodmin and King's Lynn

MANIFESTO

beatthedust press

We met in London pubs, boozers of the smoke, rub-a-dubs in King's Cross, Fleet Street, and Spitalfields. Mostly we met in Clerkenwell – the Three Kings, the Horseshoe, and The Betsey Trotwood. Fitting really. Clerkenwell – home to anarchists and rebels, protestors and rioters. The seeds of our book sprouted and grew in a pub named after a Dickens' character, fed by the ghostly Clerkenwell apparitions of Wat Tyler, William Cobbett, Tolpuddle Martyrs, Chartists, Lenin, and flash mobs, just a brick throw from the graves of William Blake and Daniel Defoe. Clerkenwell – the "headquarters of republicanism, revolution and ultra-nonconformity". So, our protest began there and continues in the form of the book you are now reading.

We have created Protest! in an attempt to define the times in which we live to those who want, and those who do not want to listen. Protest! is our homage to now.

We infect your brain like invading parasites, immunizing you against the dull and the ho-hum with cases of psychopathology, doses of feminism and cases of beer.

We protest against turgid prose and the endless repetition of storylines. Our writing is aimed at the bored and the ADHD generation.

We will not be pigeonholed, we do not believe in genre, we will not be categorized.

We write to thrill, to make you think and question. We write as a thrill and to ask ourselves why.

We WILL get your attention.

We are not insular and isolated – our stories take place in the UK, Thailand, and Australia. Our reach is global, our subjects are manifold.

We are writers doing it for ourselves — Beat the Dust Press is a small indie publisher run by a writer. We have created this book as a way of making ourselves heard, to get our words out there by whatever means possible, because we think we have something important to say.

We are individualists united by a common goal to root out the bland, the beige, and the boring.

We write from a working-class perspective, from our roots and from our boots. We are bold in our creative thinking, and keen to challenge the boundaries of writing and the subjects we write about. This is real writing for real people about the way things are now.

We are honest. We tell it like it is not like we pretend it to be. This book is an escape portal to the real.

We set free our minds and protest against logic.

We lob our stories — like word-exploding Molotov cocktails — at the gutless, and narrow-minded, and torch the "how-to" "dot-to-dot" guides of creative-writing courses.

We have no masters, rather forebears — writers, musicians and artists we like from around the world.

We write about the love of the rush, the heat of the moment, the beauty of the body, the wirings of the mind. We protest against the stupid, the unthinking, the herd. Our writing is brave, incendiary, and agitating. Our world moves at the speed of light in a web that covers the planet.

We embrace the democratizing effects of the internet, while damning the growing literary effluence it has spawned.

We march into your homes, banners unfurled that read: DO NOT ACCEPT THAT'S ALL THERE IS. THINK! THINK! THINK! PROTEST! PROTEST! PROTEST!

We tread under our boots the carcasses of suppression, repression, and oppression.

We are headstrong, writers who do not blink when the world confronts us.

We do not hide from life.

We do not hide from death.

We do not hide from madness.

We revel in the 21st century.

We write as if our lives depend on it, then we write some more.

We are two cockneys and a northerner, two men and a woman.

We are here to throw verb bombs, noun missiles, sentences that shoot from the hip, paragraphs that detonate like cluster bombs, splattering the page and your minds with words as red as blood.

We challenge you to come and have a read if you think you're hard enough.

Steve Finbow
Melissa Mann
Joseph Ridgwell

ASYLUM BEACH:

TRAVELS IN THE HETEROPTIA

BY
STEVE FINBOW

Harmony, let your name be banished from the fevered world I visit.
—Tristan Tzara

Big Buddha Beach

…large black dog beside him seems to be in similar distress; its brown eyes glassy, its breath ragged, a grey and pink tongue blackened with blood. He can see a steel fan and he waits for the relief of its draft as it turns slowly on its axis. If not for the etching of ice on the window, he would swear he was somewhere in the tropics—the air fetid and flowersome, his skin damp with the faint smell of urine, and a deeper odour of excremental decay. He watches the fan turn, notices the breeze menacing the white-plastic blinds, thawing the spider webs of ice; but the cool air never reaches him. He tries to lift his hand. Nothing happens. He can smell the dog's breath, hears the rattle somewhere in its ribcage. He tries again to lift his hand—as if someone has drawn instructions for human movement and he has learned them by rote, exactly followed the guide, for his mind traces a line from its depths to the end of invisible fingertips, a dot-to-dot of electrical charges, impulses of will, and he feels his fingerprints surge into life, their valleys and hills, their ridges and clefts, prickle with the far reaches of a life. Blood fills his arteries and veins, his cartilages and tendons snap tort, relax, release, his bones creak and whinny. Pushing his hand into the deep matted fur of the dog, S feels vomit rush into his mouth. Trying not to swallow, tears well in his eyes, and he releases the bilious stew in a torrent, strings of thick matter hanging from his chin, dripping onto his shoulders and chest. Again, he reaches for the fur. His hands grasp warm air. There is no…

…in his office on the third floor of G Wing, Dr Robert Sexton holds the phone to his ear and nods, writing something in a notebook open on his desk and then immediately striking out what he has written. Changing hands to hold the phone in his right, Sexton grips the bridge of his nose with the thumb and forefinger of his left hand and squeezes, and blinks.

"And you say no one saw him leave his room?"

The senior nurse on the other end of the line pauses before responding.

"No, Doctor, the room was checked every hour as is procedure. Nothing untoward was logged. The patient was asleep."

"And he was medicated as prescribed?"

"Yes, Doctor. The new regime was introduced a week ago. Interim tests show no adverse side effects and the patient had been participating more willingly in group sessions. In fact, Doctor Strathmore—"

"Mister…"

"Mister Strathmore left a diary note recommending the patient be allowed visitors."

"Ask Mister Strathmore to call me."

"Yes, Doctor."

"And, nurse?"

"Yes, Doctor?"

"What has Security to say about this, er, occurrence?"

"They say, Doctor, that if you treat the patients—"

"Clients, nurse."

"Yes, Doctor. If you treat the clients the way you insist on treating them that these sort of 'occurrences' are inevitable."

"Oh, they are, are they?"

"The Head of Security pointed out that they recommended checks every thirty minutes and it was you who rejected that recommendation. That you asked for the checks to be discontinued and all rooms to be left unlocked."

Doctor Sexton grips the bridge of his nose, his fingertips leaving red indentations in his pale skin.

"I will discuss this further with Mister Strathmore. Thank you, nurse."

"I'm off duty in an hour. If there's anything—"

Sexton replaces the receiver in its cradle. Shaking his head as to rebalance its workings, he looks out of the window. The palm trees with their monstrous eyelashes, the coconuts like gobs of eye gunk, their trunks the spindly limbs of some Surreal pachyderm, their…

…sat on the floor of his room tugging a thread from the woven rug heaped before him. The thread—as red and shiny as the skin on his knees—reluctant to be parted from its place in the rug's intricacies—forms thin white lines on S's fingers, which he occasionally licks in an attempt to get a firmer grip. Achieve a better purchase. The lines to the checkout tills are longer than usual for a Tuesday afternoon and S looks along the row in an attempt to find a shorter queue and, therefore, a quicker exit. His trolley, filled with cartons of milk, wedges of cheese, bricks of butter, pulls him towards the last checkout. A man in his sixties tugs and rolls produce over a sheet of glass or plastic, the beeps that signal a successful reading sound like the mating call of an insect or bird. One of the nurses—S has trouble remembering their names [Paul, Duncan, Vince]—allows him, on Thursdays, to feed the doves, their grey and petrol feathers thick with parasites and dust from the buildings their faeces slowly consume. The thread pulled free, S dangles it in front of his mouth; his short pink tongue taking wide sweeps at the thread's trajectory. The door to his room opens and The Administrator enters carrying a tray upon which S can see a scape of mugs and cups, bowls and plates, as if the whole thing were a magical plastic city floating in space.

"Thank you," S says. "You're just in time."

"As always," The Administrator says. "And how are we feeling today?"

"I'm…."

OFF/ON:
At the instant the world was born, it was divided in two. Two worlds, two planets – one was named Terra, the other they called Thule.

Dance of the Mynah Birds

…taken him a long time to not see them. The surf has drowned out the noise of their brushings, the soft creak of their branches, the dull thud of their fruits in the littered sand. But at night they haunt his dreams, striding up the beach to his bungalow, bombarding him with noise and shadow. Sexton pulls a journal from the bookshelves and flicks through the pages, his eyes stalling on photographs, illustrations, the coloured sections of the brain—the pink, the yellow, the pale blue. Stops to look at x-rays of the spinal column, its architecture resembling a cluster of copycat invertebrates joined together in a community, a colony, like coral. If the mind was his fetish—the id his Jimmy Choo sandal, the ego his latex mask, and the superego his paddle and electric node, then the body was the cesspit, the abattoir drain, the outhouse in a jungle gastroenterology unit. If S has escaped the room in which he should not have been locked into, if he has absconded from the space in which he was spied upon, that meant Sexton's methods are beginning to work. The total social rehabilitation of psychiatric patients. The acceptance of them within society—and, to begin with, within the hospital matrix. That is, to allow the 'clients' to enact and communicate their different forms of existence and thought within an accepting community. The hospital as the first stage in embracing all human 'realities'. Was S's case the first manifestation of what Sexton had argued in numerous papers, articles, and presentations? A human being whose reality is the means of escape; a human being who has, indeed, gone beyond, is existing in the without-world, is being elsewhere? S came to the hospital via…

…opens onto a cement staircase that leads both up and down from a bone-grey landing. Peering over the rail-less edge, he counts twenty, thirty flights before the steps blur into diagonals, switch back and forth until they disappear. Looking up, he sees a mirrored reflection of his previous vision. He steps onto the platform. Closing the door behind him, he tests the handle. It is self-locking. It will not open out. It will not open in. Emblazoned on the door in bright orange paint is a symbol neither number nor letter, something like a truncated U, the right arm foreshortened and topped with what looks like a fishing hook. He hadn't noticed when he had opened the door that another staircase led down from the platform directly in front of him, descending straight out into a hazy space filled with motes of light shining black and then white. He steps onto the first stair, steps down. From somewhere far beneath and far above, a footstep sounds. Descending. Ascending. He takes another step and again hears the echo. After four steps, the angle of the incline increases and he feels himself tripping down the stairs, sometimes missing one, two steps at a time, righting himself, balancing, sliding over edges until it feels as if he is moving across the unrelenting concrete, barely touching its surface, almost floating. Looking down, trying to concentrate on his seemingly controlled fall, he catches glimpses of bright-orange symbols on the walls of the adjacent staircases, some blurred and unreadable, but others burn their shapes into his retinas. Just as he feels himself to be falling headlong, now out of control, his descent endlessly accelerating, until he slows and his bare feet feel the infinitesimal grains of the concrete, and he hears the slap of his soles, hears the echoes on the steps above and below him. A platform appears as he stops to rest, his breath shallow, a light perspiration on his upper lip and forehead. To his left, a door opens; on it is painted the truncated U symbol. He tries the handle. This time, it turns. He opens the door. The passageway leads…

…bearded, paunchy, dressed in a cheap suit bought from a tailor on Singapore's Orchard Road, he smiles as he replaces the receiver. Staring at a patient's flow chart on his desk, Michael

Strathmore cracks his knuckles as he thinks about the imminent meeting with Doctor Sexton. As Administrator, Strathmore has slowly changed the ideology of Villa 21. Doctor Sexton, short on funds, desperately trying to continue with his ideal, his idea to treat psychiatric patients in a free and open environment, has handed over administrative control to Strathmore and he, a whiz with applications and grants, has steadied the floundering ship, introducing security guards, locked rooms, medication, patients' records, and most of this without Sexton's agreement. Sexton, increasingly ensconced in his office, honing his vision of an integrated society in which (in Strathmore's view) the psychotic, the mentally disturbed, the schizophrenic, and the insane, are treated as if their illnesses, their afflictions, their hells, are mere common ailments, are treated (again in Strathmore's view) like minor celebrities, free-thinkers, embodiments of karma and grace, visionaries even. Strathmore dials Sexton's number, pushes the speaker button.

"You wanted to see me, Doctor Sexton?"

"Yes. Are you free now?"

"Give me an hour. I have a few things to finish."

"OK. Two o'clock, my office."

Strathmore puts down the phone, sits in his black office chair, puts his feet up on his desk, closes his…

He awoke and wanted Thule. The touch of its fine blue soil. The cool sun like a smudged fingerprint. The snug fit of his respirator. The taste of the Thulean air filtered through the stabilizer. The twin moons—Shlerma and Kogona—racing in the Thulean sky. He jacked into the Inf. Spoke the unspoken name. Would he always have to go back this way?

The Story of the For-Real Bird and the Disapproval Bird

…up in the coconut palms, the Disapproval Bird and the For-Real Bird are having a conversation.

"Tut! Tut! Tut!" says the Disapproval Bird.

"For-Real! For-Real!" says the For-Real Bird.

The Disapproval Bird has a small beak, tightly closed except, of course, when eating the vibrantly white moths upon which it feeds. The For-Real Bird has a long yellow and black beak with two ridges on the top and bottom coloured a lobstery red. The For-Real Bird gapes in the heat. Its shit—electric green from the berries it eats—dries a dull brown and covers the base of the tree in which the two birds perch.

"Tut! Tut! Tut!" says the Disapproval Bird.

"For-Real! For-Real!" says the For-Real Bird.

As the For-Real Bird turns its head, within the moment of its blink, it witnesses a grey world, windows covered with bars, no handles on the doors, a metal bed frame topped with a thin mattress and the mattress covered with a rubber sheet. A six-inch long bare electrical flex holds an energy-saving bulb that looks like a clenched fist. The room smells of medicine and bleach, smells both human and metallic.

"Tut! Tut! Tut!" says the Disapproval Bird.

"For-Real! For-Real!" says the For-Real Bird.

Puffing up its turquoise and black feathers, the Disapproval Bird shakes its head, lifts its right leg to scratch at the parasites lodged in its bristling chest. The parasites huddle together, emitting high-pitch screams, sonically embedding themselves in the Disapproval Bird's skin. Pulling out a beak-full of chest feathers, the pain a relief from the constant itching, the Disapproval Bird finds himself strapped to a wooden table, bright lights shine in his eyes, oversized instruments in precise rows on a metal tray. An invisible hand lifts the sharpest of these implements. The Disapproval Bird sees the glint of its fine blade, the tooled criss-cross etchings on its handle, feels the first incision in its tiny skull.

"Tut! Tut! Tut!" says the Disapproval Bird.

"For-Real! For-Real!" says the...

...office window, Sexton can barely make out the hunched shoulders of Koh Phangan. Lost in the heat haze, the island flashes on and off in his vision, as if short-circuiting, its peaks and beaches spectral realities on an ever-shifting horizon.

Two sharp knocks shake the doctor from his daydreams.

"Come in."

Michael Strathmore opens the door and strides into the centre of Sexton's office, sits down without being asked.

"Doctor," he says as if reaffirming Sexton's existence.

"Michael. Anything more on the disappearance?"

"Not really. As you know, the patient was admitted a week ago. Your colleagues in London diagnosed him as a severe paranoiac with episodes of dementia followed by intense euphoria resulting in spontaneous and multiple orgasms. Your treatment seemed to exacerbate rather than control the, er, mental instability."

"On the contrary. If the client was able to escape from your locked room and evade your elaborate security systems, then his periods of lucidity must have increased and his paranoid dementia decreased. My treatment, as you call it, I prefer the word 'understanding,' appears to have been successful."

"But now the patient—sorry, client—is free and somewhere on the island. Who's to say he will not have a relapse and, confronted by unfamiliar surroundings, become violent?"

"Paranoia, dementia, euphoria, orgasm followed or preceded by a period of calm. I used extreme pornography to accelerate the orgasmic stage, bypassing the paranoia/dementia phase. Keeping the client in a perpetual euphoric/orgasmic condition subverts and/or suppresses any violence caused by the eliding back into paranoia/dementia. No drugs, Michael. No invasive surgery." Sexton looks above Strathmore's head at a photo on his office wall showing Sexton as a student in the company of R.D. Laing and David Cooper.

"I have informed the local police," Strathmore says.

"What about your own security?"

"They're investigating. Four of them are looking for the escapee. I very much doubt he has managed to leave the island."

"When he is found, I want him returned here. In the meantime, all rooms are to be opened, all non-essential medication is to be stopped, and the clients will be allowed to use the gardens and the pools."

"Do you think that's wise, Doctor?"

"It is my decision, Michael."

"I'll see to it right away."

"And, no doubt, you will be reporting to the board."

"As I said, Doctor, it is your decision."

"My rounds will be at 4 p.m., please inform the nursing staff."

Strathmore rises, cracks his knuckles, and leaves the office. Sexton looks out of the window. The sea—a dead calm—barely laps against…

…thought at first it was the torn off corner of a sachet of coffee or green tea, or the ragged triangular tip of a burned leaf, but he realizes after a while that what he is watching is the struggling body of a dying butterfly, its wings folded, legs kicking against the water, kicking against the pull of the waves. He blinks, the salt water stinging his eyes, abrading his tongue and throat. The butterfly's antennas still and its surprisingly large body stops its convulsions and, in what feels like a shrug, both man and butterfly are pitched onto the shore. The sand, alive with busy crabs and lazy flies, dead with rotting leaves and dried dog shit, is gritty and coarse, made sharp with fragments of shell and coral, tin cans and broken beer bottles. The swim, from what he can remember, had been less arduous than he had imagined. He had used up most of his energy in the push from the beach, swimming out under the waves until he felt the water temperature change, the sea floor drop away beneath him, and the current pull him out into the channel. There was light from the squid fishing boats, the stars, and the towns dotted along the islands' shores. In the daylight, he can see that he hasn't reached his goal. The island he has washed up on is a smaller one—like a caesura between the two main islands. He hasn't eaten since the day before yesterday, a thin aromatic soup he drained in one long swallow, the chillies burning his throat, tearing his eyes. What had caused the butterfly to drown? Was it his fault? His body causing turbulences and pressure changes, his head a small mountain, his legs framing a tucked inlet, the valley of his navel creating rain clouds, his body's thermal…

The Heteroptia Consul sat on the balcony of the ebony spaceship and wondered what he was to do with the retrogade S. The man had absconded from the Zeitzone, had killed three of his best agents. They were sure he had been heading for Thule, but a lock down and search of that miserable planet's cities yielded nothing but gossip and misinformation. S had to be somewhere in the Solsys—he couldn't stay away from Thule forever.

The Abandoned Staircase

…towards the hospital. He keys in the pass number, the automatic doors slide open. The lobby is cool, air-conditioned. The staff's clothing approximating uniforms. All-white clothing is not allowed. The only sound is that of their rubber-soled shoes squeaking on the highly polished floor. A sign hangs above the curvilinear desk. At first, he is unable to read it, and then the letters form into recognisable shapes: RECEPTION. A light sweat breaks out on his forehead and upper lip. He steps up to the desk, its two occupants busy, their heads down, their fingers punching keys seemingly at random. A third stands behind them flicking through files in a grey metal cabinet. He swallows. Words trapped somewhere in his body, fleeing from the air, the light, intestinal. The people at the desk simultaneously look up, noticing him for the first time.

"My name is…"

They stare at him, look at each other. One of them picks up a phone, says something in a language he does not recognize, the stream of sound is full of plosives. He looks up at the sign, it reads TRVR{YOPM. A hand grasps his arm. He closes his eyes. Nods. The elevator doors open…

TAPED REPORT OF CLIENT "S" PREPARED BY DR SEXTON—03/06/XX: AUTOBIOGRAPHY (I) …rarely visit my hometown. Not, as you might think because of any childhood trauma, but because it is a dreary place, soulless, without grace. During the day, the concrete and glass shopping centre is full of people filing in and out of the charity shops, the supermarkets, the local pubs; while, at night, the latter bristle with a barely restrained violence. My parents had recently died—a car accident on the coast road near Torrox in Spain—and I had returned to their home to collect papers my brother had put aside. The church steeple of St. Catherine's—

once known as Feltham's Folly—is attached to a social-security benefits office, the vestry having been destroyed by fire in the seventies, and the whole thing looks cobbled together, hobbled together, like a racehorse pulling a cart full of children's building blocks. Alongside the old church, runs a man-made river built to provide water for Hampton Court or something like that. I can't remember exactly. I once knew the history. Once knew the town. The river—Long-ford—offered itself to childhood adventures: inflated inner-tubes transformed into pirate corsairs, Drake's Golden Hind, Nelson's Victory, Cook's Endeavour, the rubber dinghies used in night raids on German-held French beaches by Commandoes, their faces camouflaged, or Terran troops lost somewhere on Thule, the blue soil burning through their exo-suits. The river flows through the neighbouring towns, grey places, Bedfont and Hanworth. Sometimes trips along its length became battles. Gangs of children, spears made from sharpened branches, threw stones, whips fashioned from saplings, slingshots made from supple tree forks. I remember cutting open my foot on a shard of green glass—it was under 'the first bridge' as we called it. The fish—mostly sticklebacks and gudgeon—snapping at the flowing blood. I remember newts, crested and not, the sexual rush of stinging nettles, and the magic salve of dock leaves. Where the Prince of Wales pub once stood, a 24-hour drive-in McDonald's blares away. The notorious outside lavatories of the old pub were hunting grounds for giant spiders and pederasts. Opposite the McDonald's is the shell of another pub—The Feltham Hotel. Here, from my early teens into my late, from bunking off school until I worked in a carpet shop in the precinct, I spent my time drinking lager and feeding the flashing and beeping, the rarely burping and spewing fruit machines. I sometimes won, much to the scowling disapprobation of the barman whose name—at least, the one we called him by—was Spamhead. In my late teens, my friends and I started a con—a way to cheat Spamhead and the pub out of, what was to us at the time, expensive beer. The pub's bar was horseshoe-shaped, a large mirror running down its middle. If Spamhead was on the far side of the bar, he could not see customers on the nearside facing the door. After we'd nearly finished our first set of drinks, one of us—Paul, Brian, Dennis or myself—would walk to the far-side bar and order a round, while the others went to the near-side and topped up their original pints from the pumps. This must've been around the late seventies. I think the pub closed in the early…

…through the wreckage, the discarded things. Rusted water tanks, white goods soiled by heat and rain, broken fridges, abandoned microwaves, the sad gap-toothed smile of unwanted chessboards. An odd sensation, almost embarrassment, a blush rises on his cheeks at the disregard we have for inanimate objects, mere paraphernalia. He wishes everything, every thing, could be fetishized: sofas, the smallest microbe, the lurid covers of a cheap science-fiction novel; a metastases of human and non-human obsessions. He masturbates about a Perspex goldfish bowl, while you slip in and out of your vagina, your anus, a plastic toy you found by the kerbside. He wanks over the steel shutters of the shop opposite, while you stroke your breasts, your perineum, with a fly pupae. His black patent-leather shoes burn in the tropical sun. He snatches them off and avidly takes them to your pure white buttocks. The lubrication on the ashtray eases its egress. The Administrator notes the expression on their faces, the boredom and the surprise. The film…

The Heteroptia Consul belongs to an elite order, a hallowed subcategory. The man delivers. Simstims. Neural enforcers. Synaptic syntax like you'd never believe. You want Thule? You got it. You want that third eye so fashionable on Tchitcherine 3? He will deliver. He came on the mothership way back in the day, when the earth still had water and her inhabitants barely knew of Thule.

Song of the Crickets

TAPED REPORT OF CLIENT "S" PREPARED BY DR SEXTON 03/06/XX—AUTOBIOGRAPHY (II) …cuboid shopping centre faces into an expanse of paving slabs once book-ended by fountains neither of which I ever saw work. The scars of their presence still visible in the broken concrete and the stopped water pipes. Opposite the precinct's one remaining pub is a Superdrug store shining whitely. This was once a carpet shop where, for two years or so, I worked as a salesman. The store sold carpets, rugs, linoleum, wood flooring and—on the first floor—beds. Occasionally, I would bring girlfriends back to the closed store late at night and fuck them on the new mattresses, my coke-and-speed-hardened cock working selfishly away at the ever-desiccating vaginas. I remember one girl's nails, bitten and cracked, painted a crab pink. But I don't remember her name. I do recall that my foreskin reeked of cock cheese and the way she gagged when I pulled her head down to my aching cock. Another girl, whose mother disapproved of me, and from whom I stole a copy of De Quincey's *Confessions of an English Opium-Eater* and an anthology of modern poetry, I fucked on a roll of underfelt. One day, when the shop was empty of customers and I was sitting in the office at the back of the store slowly easing the point of a compass into a fold of skin at the top of my left testicle, two young men, about my age, entered the shop. I recognized one of them from my old school on Thule, teeth as yellow as his hair, the hair hanging unwashed over a knitted brow, shifty, eyes focused down and to the side, clothes second-hand and ill-fitting. The second man, vaguely familiar, taller and broader, with a more purposeful if less-intelligent face, hung back in the doorway.

"All right, S?" the first young man said.

"All right, Tony? What do you want?" I said, closing the till, locking it, and walking out of the office.

"Nothing to do with me," he said motioning with his head back towards the other man.

"Get out of the shop," I said.

"Don't forget. It's got nothing to do with me."

"What hasn't?"

He put his head down and again gestured towards the man in the doorway.

"S?" he said.

"Yeah," I said.

"Remember me?"

"No. Should I?"

"Peter Worth," he said.

"So?" I said, recognizing him now as another member of my class, one who barely attended school.

"I've just got out and I'm paying back everyone who bullied me."

I couldn't remember bullying him. I wasn't a bully. I did remember being dismissive of his presence—when he was present—an existence that hardly registered, a non-being forever absent even when he was there, a waste of memory.

"Look. I work here. If you've got a problem with me, you'll have to wait. But now get out or I'll call the Terra-squad."

I was on my own. My colleague, on a break, was not due back for a while.

"Outside," he said in a spray of anger and cliché.

I stepped…

…strangle the dog, its constant yapping instantly turns into birdsong, its being lost on the tropical breeze. An ant races across the arctic white of the page, fleeing the cover's avalanche. He sits, his legs burning from mosquito bites and too much exposure to the sun. His beer warming in the afternoon heat, his brain frying with words as numerous and insistent as insects. The ant reaches the bottom right-hand corner of the page, confronted with the page number's infinitesimal ridges, it halts, rubs its antennae together…

…in a bamboo gazebo drinking beer, reading a science-fiction thriller about some abscondee from Ultima Thule lost in the ever-enfolding, unfolding, infolding realms of space-time, pursued by agents, The Administrator, and The Heteroptia Consul, but secretly staring above the pages at a girl in a tiny black bikini standing knee-deep in the waves reading a book by Ursula Le Guin. The girl's tight shorts ride up her buttocks revealing a perfect arse, tanned and firm, the gap between her thighs forms an egg of bright blue seawater. She has small high breasts, quite masculine shoulders, and a line around her neck lighter than the rest of her skin as if she were marked out for some future execution. As his eyes drop down from the vision to the page, he reads, "Doctor Sexton set down his antique pen and jacked into the Inf. The Administrator was at fault. Didn't he know to report everything to him? He was the Heteroptia Consul—Primary Object. How had S escaped? He had killed a Tchitcherine priest, an agent-familiar, and possibly a young Terran girl. Reports say he is still on one of the islands while some unconfirmed sightings place him in Bangkok." He looks up as a young girl, ten or eleven years old, steps out of the sea on tiptoe, her newly formed breasts glistening. Through the fabric of his swimming trunks, he strokes his cock and watches the setting sun and the horizon like a scalpel line drawn through a rotting peach. The girl spreads her young body on a towel, turns her palms…

There was a time, half a million years ago or so, when some new neighbours came into the vicinity of the earth's solar system—Solsys. Because of their near-perfect ability to integrate with the Terrans, their presence was merely hinted at in historical records, myths of blood type, of lycanthropes and vampires, of Thuleans walking amongst us. S jacked further into the sys, felt his blood boil, his two brains meld into one, his hyperspine running with Inf.

The Empty Pool

…leads to a platform that leads to another staircase then another platform, from this, constructed of cement, the staircase descends, almost depends, the wooden steps suspended in midair. As far as he can tell, the stairs are leading him nowhere, the door he entered from, now invisible behind him, yet there is no visible exit just more stairs descending and ascending. But over what? Under what? Maybe people live in the spaces carved out beneath the shapes formed by the stairs—ziggurats, Mayan pyramids, ocean trenches. He stops on a platform dizzy from the heat, his thoughts. The space above his head sometimes claustrophobic, the ceiling brushing his hair; sometimes vast and within which he imagines his breath forming giant clouds or nimbus universes. The light comes from nowhere, everywhere, glows around him, showing him snatches of riser and step, platforms and floors, a wall painted with swastikas and mandalas. He wipes the sweat from his eyes, blinks, steps off from the platform, drops vertiginously. He lifts his arms out to steady his descent, taking one then two, then three steps at a time—school's out, daddy's home, the ice-cream man is here—faster, further, almost flying. Then. Stop. White on red. Red on white. EXIT. He pushes open the door. The air outside is hot, hotter than the stairwell. He is in an alley. Shops selling T-shirts, shorts, sun hats, others selling food, drinks. The alley is a covered one. The cover made from reed matting. He steps. Halfway along the alley of shops is a recess. Within the recess, he sees a platform, bare canvas for a floor, ropes strung at hip height around its four sides, each corner padded, the ropes swinging noiselessly as if someone had just climbed over or through them. The ring is empty. The space smells of chemicals and sweat, liniment and blood. He steps in. At the far end of the recess a curtain opens and he hears a man cough and a hand…

…on top of the cool white sheets listening to the air-conditioning unit. The noise sounds like the clatter of a million horses, a multitude of extraterrestrial horses, eight-limbed, twenty-four limbed, a hundred-limbed, alien millipedal horses, armoured in keratin and steel, in amber and verdigris, their manes made from rope and sand, seaweed and chewing gum, blazing in the molten Thulean wind, gleaming in the broken sun, their hooves on fire like falling fighter planes, like firebirds of the netherworld, sparks flying up from the cobbled streets, from the edges of the waves laid down like countless antimacassars on the broad shoulders of the beach. On top of the cool white sheets listening to the air-conditioning unit, the incoherent words, the untenable sacrifices, the suicides, the multiple layers of wallpaper soaked in…

…fly hit the tiles and looks down to see it spinning. After a while, it stops and rights itself, flips again on its back, then on to its legs. It stands, takes a faltering step, another, stops, its two back legs playing over the rear end of its fluorescent green body, then delicately lifts a pair of translucent wings to dry in the sun. Using its two front legs, the fly wipes its large red compound eyes, and then wipes its proboscis, testing, tasting its newfound reality. Its abdomen is humbug striped. The fly remains motionless for a few minutes then takes to the air, slamming into the glass doors of his room. It falls to the floor and is immediately besieged by a group of red ants, phenomena of order in the chaos of his unconscious. The ants crawl over…

In the shadows of the forest that flanks the cyanic plain by the Lost Sea of Korus in the Valley Dor, beneath the hurtling moons of Thule, S hides his meta-suit beneath a rock shaped like a human head. His body camoufaceted to mimic the planet's cyanic earth, he looks out at the sweeping plain and plots his revenge. His destiny. The Heteroptia is coming down.

The War Between the Ants

…of his past, he looks at the pale trace of the moons in the afternoon sky. What he is looking at is the past. The past. As naked as fireworks, the railway lines of his limbs, the description of everything. Just that. What he sees is a likening to what it was. What it is. The palm trees. "The palm trees." [The palm trees.] The condensation on the beer can. {The condensation on the beer can.} The ants—The ants—Because he can imagine he can imagine. Or: because he could imagine he could imagine. The words are not the same every time he writes them down. The words are not the same. Every time he writes them down. The words are not the same every time. He writes them down. Not the same. The same. The fifty-something woman's breasts, oiled, her nipples infolded like knife slits, vicious laughter, dangerous smiles. And he looks at her teeth, crooked, holding each other up like drunken sugar cubes. Her eyes hidden behind giant sunglasses. "Insects," he thinks. Those who kill their mates. Sex—the foreplay of death. Language its shadowy chaperone. The moons slip in the sky, the people rush to…

…cataractic iris of the blue-eyed afternoon sun. The beach smells of latrines: fish-head beach, dog-turd beach, dead-crab beach. Stones that are teeth. Shells that are red-meat chrysalides. Sand the woollen hat pulled tight over bleached-skull beach. He sits in a wooden chair just to one side of the pool. He reads for a while and then jots down observations and thoughts in a striped notebook. Something to do with the light, the shade, the changing positions of the four people on the sun-loungers—each lounger has a number engraved on a brass plate screwed to the front of its wooden frame: 1789, 1961, 1459, 2108. When he looks again, he realizes that the first woman resembles someone he had known at university—her thighs are fatter, her breasts smaller—but the way she raises her hand to shade out the sun reminds him of the way… (Yes,

Caroline was her name) …warded off his shouts, his blows, and the way the woman struggles out of her sweat-soaked T-shirt mirrors the way Caroline huddled in the corner, her arms raised, her body foetal, to block his punches, his kicks. He stands and strolls toward the pool, the cement path burning the soles of his feet, the four people oblivious to his approach. He splashes through the foot pool, stops at the water's edge, turns to face the woman.

"Caroline," he says, assertive not interrogative. "Caroline."

The woman opens her eyes. The three other sunbathers turn their heads to look at him.

"Caroline," he says.

The woman shakes her head and answers in a language he does not at first understand but, slowly, as if finding a familiar station on a radio, the words become clear, concise, undissolved granules of sugar at the bottom of a cup of coffee.

And she says, "something is missing. Not visible. It grew bigger and I explained. White holes. All kinds of passages."

He nods, reaches out a hand. The man sitting next to the woman stands, steps forward, says something. The septum…

"…idea what things really are, no idea of any human state; nothing in this world turns for me, nothing turns in me. Being alive, I suffer horribly. I fail to reach any existing state." Sexton looks at his notes, reads, "Dead to the world; dead to that which is for everyone else the world, fallen at last, fallen, uplifted in the void I once refused, I have a body that submits to the world, and disgorges reality." Sexton runs his right index finger across the page, lifts it…

The sky above the port was the colour of television tuned to a dead channel. He dropped the last of his sonarcotics, the instant soundtrack pumping through his nervous system—meteorites burning up in Thule's thin atmosphere, the sound of distant cyrnbals set upon by robots yielding metal hammers, the resonant sound of the grajabpi plucked by a master musician. The morph-ine slowly, imperceptibly, changed his facial structure until, as he reached the doors of the Heteroptia Consulate, he was infused with power.

Butterflies and Blood

…underslung clouds, limpet pink, gelatinous, reflect back the light from the water. Fishermen and women sit up to their necks, filtering the sand for shellfish. The waves. His cock through the cheap fabric of his shorts, he watches the girl in the green bikini. Her skin is a uniform honey colour, devoid of any perspiration, while his runs with rivulets of sweat. From the stem, shaved of all hair, his cock hardens, pumped with blood, his veins and arteries thickening, darkening, the glans purple above the roseate length, and he feels his whole being forced there, the plant budding, the spaceship on its final approach. She sits up, her small breasts tipped with biscuit-coloured nipples. Her hair tied back, blonde. He strokes his cock, which, to his disbelief, grows harder, becomes the size of him, of the pier he looks out on, of the world. Her arms outstretched, upturned. Her knees raised creating triangles, arches, pyramids. He gets to his feet, slips off his shorts and, while walking towards her, masturbates. The air between them pulling him forward. No breeze. Her eyes closed, sweet skinned, the perfect hillock of her sex, the bikini bottoms cut like lime between the toffee, sharp lines of her thigh muscles. Almost ceremoniously, primal, before the worlds and the word, he stands before her, his shadow lost in the noon sun, invisible, he spurts his semen on her breasts and neck, comes again on her chin, and again onto and into her open mouth, the colour of his come the colour of her teeth. She opens her eyes, looks up at his cock, screams at the sight and touch of his opalescent gift. The tattoo girdling her…

…his eyes. The space confined, almost within him. A cell. The cell. Within the cell. And the cells make up in their entirety—the cellar—a collection of cells. And the doctor's office is the nucleus. But if the office is the nucleus, what is the doctor? He closes his eyes. He feels as though he is rocking, adrift on the sea, semi-conscious on a Thai fisherman's boat, naked, burning in the heat, the smell of the sea, the smell of the catch, of wood smoke and ozone, of his own stench. He turns on his side and vomits on the floor, splashing his shoulder with a reek of sourness and sugar, of chillies and garlic, of the bottom of the sea. He reaches out and feels the wall, clammy with humidity. How is he back here? The near silence of the waves. The muffled roar of the engine. The quiet of the walls. The oppressive weight of the hospital above. The archaeology of cloaca…sebum…blood…semen…stamen…bulb… acrid…acid…

…waiting over an hour at the junction of the two roads. His scalp tingles with the heat of the sun. His mouth dry, his tongue searches for moisture. Thirty minutes into the second hour, he sees the young priest, his saffron robes bright against the dull concrete buildings. The priest turns right towards the beach town, away from the mountains, the jungle. He stands, waits for the priest to pass. Follows. The priest walks slowly, head down. He finds it difficult to maintain the pace behind, constantly stopping, waiting, and following. Taxi drivers sound their horns, slow down for him, gesture, but he ignores them, or dismisses them with a shake of his head. He tracks the priest past restaurants and cafes, massage parlours and convenience stores, past hotels and apartment complexes until the town fizzles out in a guttering of dilapidated buildings, skeletal constructions, which, in turn, become pale hills bare of trees. The traffic is lighter here and he increases his pace to catch up with the…

He has no material power as the god-emperors had; he has only a following of desert people and fishermen. The desert people are the real Thuleans—their skin sand-blasted to match the planet's hue, their dislike of oxygen, their abhorrence of all things Terra. The fishermen came to the planet with the pioneer ships. They searched for water on the barren planet, drilled into its centre, found nothing. Fishermen came to him—S—the desert people sort his guidance. His word was to accept the Terrans. They did so. They became one. They became Thuleans.

Dog-Skull Beach

…in thought or prayer, the young priest does not turn on hearing his approach, but keeps on walking, head bowed. S waits for the scooters, cars, and tuk-tuks to thin and waits again until the road closes in on the beach, and then he hurls himself at the priest, knocking him into the sparse vegetation that separates the road from the shore, man from nature. They roll down the incline, among beer bottles and plastic soft-drink containers, cigarette butts and used condoms. Man is here after all. He holds the priest with both arms, grips the priest's legs with his own, the clutch almost sexual, becoming in every roll, every turn, more so, until they both come to a stop, panting among the scattering crabs and bewildered beach dogs that bark and dart into the waves, sniff the air, paw the sand, and nervously…

…forgotten how to climb. He stands, legs apart, grounded, in front of the trifurcated trunk of a cashew tree, its fruit swaying in the breeze. Using a parasitic tendril as their highway, a liquorice line of red ants ceaselessly ascends and descends. He leans forward and watches their progress. A clot of ants carry what looks like a chicken bone up into a bole that sits between two of the limbs. The ants' journey is a slow one, determined, dogged, if ants could be those things. He places a finger into the traffic, feels the tickle of a knot of ants. Bringing his finger to his lips, he sucks the ants into his mouth, bites down. He can feel the ants bite back, swallows down the cough-syrup-coloured insects. Once he is sure his stomach acids are destroying the heads, the abdomens, the thoraxes, dissolving the legs, destroying the pincers, he reaches into the branches, takes a firm hold, and lifts himself into the heart of the tree; his hands and feet like fruit, his knees, elbows, and knuckles mirroring the boles and scars, his legs and arms the branches, his torso a fourth dimension, his eyes the flickering light between the leaves, his voice the shifting breeze the almost imperceptible creaks and groans. Into his mouth, into his ears, his nostrils, into his anus, crawl the bees, the solitary wasps, the lumbering beetles, into his urethra slithers a giant centipede. Still, he watches the sunbathers, the swimmers, the resort and hospital staff. From his camouflaged crucifixion he watches the young woman turn on her sun-bed exposing her small breasts paler than the rest of her exposed body, watches as a spider…

…walks among the blossoms, the bungalow lamps illuminating the palm trees, and a flickering light shines in the kidney-shaped pool, the water reflecting onto the large hand-shaped leaves of a parasitic climbing plant. He climbs down from the tree, steals a pair of flip-flops from the porch of the nearest bungalow, shorts from another, a T-shirt from the third. Dressed, he heads out onto the main road running parallel to the beach. It is mid-evening. The cicadas' chirrups do battle with the taxi horns for his…

The moment he entered the city, S was led to the Home. His guard said to him on the way, "you will not escape from here, Thulean. Not this time. The Administrator will see to that. You've seen your ugly ball of blue rock for the last time." The stranger—S—smiled. A sheen of sweat covered the guard's forehead and upper lip. S said, "how do you know it's me? How do you know you're you?" In his right hand, he crushed a phial of morph-ine. Who was he to become?

Millipede Nightmares

...stops. Breathes. The light dim and, for a second, he feels the rollercoaster rush of his insanity, the sharp drop, the slow rise through nothingness, the weeping turn into non-being, the plunge into darkness, so intense that it invades him, his body first and then his mind—he tries to think: open eyes, walk, enter, smile, ask, receive, swallow, breathe and he gets nightdress, appropriate, cello, about, as, expected, since, pressure—all at once, overlaid, synchronic, embedded and then he gets pt, src, dsypx, ctsmnf, and then ㅎ, θ, ㅜ, 새, π and he can hear his teeth grinding, hears the enamel chip and splinter, shear off to reveal a rough centre, jagged edges, and his teeth come together again, shatter, the nerve ends setting off sparks of raw pain and he screams. The light sharpens and he hears:

"You want play some pool?" A young girl, her…

...the bar. There are three pool tables. Three men and three young women move around the table in a slow dance. The girls bend provocatively, their tight skirts riding up over their brown buttocks. Two of the girls wear flat sandals, their legs chubby. Some have a roll of baby fat around their middles, their small breasts cupped in bikini tops, self-mutilated T-shirts. Other girls, taller, more angular, high cheekbones, fuller jaws, and these girls seem to wear more make-up, to prance and preen, to play better pool. Three other men sit or stand at the bar, each with an arm around a young girl's waist. The men wear the sun's effects like a badge, a medal—various shades of white, pink, red, and brown paint their skins. All have tattoos on various parts of their bodies. A bulging calf shows a Maori design, a name is circled by an Egyptian ankh symbol. Biceps are adorned with red, gold, and green koi, or are encircled by barbed wire or expressionist flowers. Two more men, their skin sun-and-sand-blasted, brick red, sit at the front of the bar, a girl on each knee. Yet another man leaves the bar trailing a teenage girl behind him. They leave on a scooter. The girl's arms encircling the man's bloated waist as he pulls…

…soap, chimney soot, powdered lobster claw, an underlying scent of sweat, a burp of Coca-Cola, something alcoholic. The girl is small, her head resting on his sternum. Her hair is as dark as disgrace, as shiny as crow's teeth. He thinks. His whole body perspires under the cool draft from the air-conditioning unit. She looks up at him, her eyes intoxicating yet dull, urgent yet seeing beyond her time with him, as if he were incidental, excluded from her history. She is wearing a white bikini top emphasizing her melanite skin undercut with cinnamon and primrose. Her shorts are denim and eponymous. Her shoes, he notices last, are black mules with low heels, and he can see the edges of the soles of her feet, as pale as dead leaves. What lurks in the…

A screaming comes across the sky. It has happened before, but there is nothing to compare it to now. The glass and chrome walls of the Heteroptia Consulate (Home) spider web and bend, huge shards of mirrors fall to the sidewalk, bodies—both Terra and Thulean—fall grasping the air, kicking wildly. S, the sonarcotic turned to max, a mass of white noise, marauding bass and pumped up metal-machine music, slips past the security cameras. Playback would show a shadow of a mirage of a phantom.

Red and Black and Blood and Tar

…arrived at the final station. The sign indicating its name is written in a language he does not understand. He cannot name the flowers hanging from the wire baskets, their colours from a yet unclassified spectrum. The vehicle that brought him here has long-since departed. There are no guards. No future passengers. Each time he looks at the name of the station on the sign it changes, shifting blocks of print, lengthening, shortening. The rails on which he surely travelled recede into the distance on both sides. He thinks that there may be hills but he cannot see any. The horizon is indistinct. He thinks that there may be birds but it is just the motes in his eye, forming, ever-falling, rising—gulls, terns, sea eagles, firebirds of the netherworld. His thought does not conform to things. Does not confirm. Or the reverse. The obverse. Perverse. The small stones under the rails are living things, intimate and intricate. The rails themselves planted with the immediate. The single platform of silence and communion. The galvanized iron roof of the stationhouse. Beneath a handless clock, he sees a barrel. He walks towards it. As he does, he feels the surface of things shudder, slide, slur. He looks into the barrel filled to the brim with a substance he is sure is not water. Is it liquid? Matter? In the reflection, he sees a face, his face, immediately obscured by ripples, circles spreading into, not out of the centre. The sky fades to a…

…know the names of the girls. He has asked. Ask again. Their replies are lost on their tongues, between their teeth, gristle, fibre. To them, he is who he pretends to be: Paul, Simon, Joe. He knows he does not form a part of their society, not of the men, not of the young women, not the chairs, the pool table, the mirror ball. He does not want to be part of it. He is there and not there. They are here but not here. Not there during the act. Not they during the act. Not their during the act. What is on sale is apartness, being in the not-with-world. What is on offer is physical, thisness, haeccity. A distance in presence. A future in the present. An escape into their own…

…at himself in the mirror. His face lost among the etchings of gods and monsters, of a beast with a hundred heads, of snakes with monstrous fangs, blue-headed demons, dog-men, women with palms closed into fists, eyes shut, heads down, vulture-men, men with glass abdomens, a woman with the body of a spider; a waiting room for humanity, aspects of the non-human, the animal, the divine, the abhorrent and the desired. And there he is. He sees the back of his head reflected back at him. But that is not possible. He turns to the left and the face in the mirror turns to the right. Snaps back. He grips the bar. The girl holds his arm. The music slows, blurs, a stricken note plays repeatedly. The mirror ball slows to a halt, shines silver and red, gold and green. Spins again—faster and faster, the music now matching its beat. His heart, compulsive, jerks him awake. He thrusts his head towards the mirror, stares into his eyes, pokes out his tongue, flares his nostrils, sees: monkey, ape, hyena, jackal, pig, dog, weasel; sees: a halo, sees a lizard, snake, sees a mass of buzzing insects where his head should be; sees static, whiteout, snow. Does not see…

They shipped him into exile in the cheapest kind of Tchitcherine drogue. For two days, he was blind and deaf, stunned with drugs, his body packed in a thick matrix of deceleration paste, his dreams wired into the Heteroptia's Retrovision—remaking his history, giving him a family when there was not one. A grey and boring hometown, an unexciting life. Long gone. The inftendrils reached deep into his body, coursed through his veins and arteries, surged through his nervous system, restructuring neural pathways, decombinant, altering his very being—tables that are boa constrictors, the chairs that surround the snakes alphabets, recipes for words.

Speedboat to Nowhere

…sprawled on wooden flooring. He tries to raise his head but his neck muscles do not respond to his promptings. He tries again. He is in some kind of basement, cellar, dungeon. Painfully, he manages to lift his head. There is no light. There is no sound. He sits with his back against a wall, urging himself to remember. The room is cold. The dark is thinning but more in presence than perception.

"Hey!" he shouts. "Hello!"

He reaches out an arm, towards what he isn't sure. The darkness shrinks, contains itself, and then surrounds. How did he get to this place? Wherever he was before, he has managed to not be there, he is now here. In the middle of what? In the middle of where? His head throbs with pain and he's not sure if it is caused by something internal, as if his brain—in its animal way—were punishing him for neglecting to know, to consider, to remedy and to reason. How will he conciliate his own mind, console it? Maybe the pain was caused by something external: brick, pipe, head—so intimate, so immediate, so effective.

His body is in the hands of strangers. Stranger. For an hour? Two? A week? Months? Whatever happens to him is already over. What is happening is a matter of time. Just that. What will happen to him is impossible to know. Has. Is. Will. Has is will. But now. Now can never be too late. Becoming real…

…a tug on his arm. The tunnel. He turns. The girl looks up at him, eyes incurious. Her hands on her slim hips, her arms forming triangles, the two arcs of her breasts, the two perfect circles of her nipples, the bright white diminishing rectangles of her teeth, the oblong of her nostrils, the labyrinths of her ears, the bow-shaped spread of her…

...no sound. He strains to listen. It is not silence but there is no sound. Or the nothing between sounds. He bangs on the wall with his fists.

"Hey!" he shouts. "Hello! Someone!"

A light goes on causing him to close his eyes. Blinking, he sees a man holding a metal tray.

"Your arm," The Administrator says.

"What?"

The man kneels in front of him. He pushes back against the wall willing it to yield, to be what it is not, cannot be. The man is smiling, his lips parted, his teeth together, lines forming on his cheeks, his eyes radiating spokes of folded skin.

"Your arm," The Administrator says, "or we will have to constrain you."

He extends his left arm, makes a fist. Recall. Instinct. Repetition. He grimaces. A reaction at least. Why is he compliant? Is this man here to hurt or heal? Is he here to take him from this cell? Is he here to take him home? Wherever that may be. Maybe. Is. Thule. Terra.

Behind the kneeling man, he sees another man. Vaguely familiar. This man speaks to the kneeling man in a language that sounds like it has been constructed of children's building blocks dropped onto a tiled floor. He tries to stand. Tries to understand. Tries to say something to the two men. There is a long silent plunge into darkness. There is no longer...

The place had to be some sort of old hotel or resort or something. There were big-toothed metal wheels half buried in the wooden floors or hanging by giant spindles from the network of iron beams overhead. Both Terrans and Thuleans worked the machinery, worked in the machinery, their heads and spinal columns forming the wetware that drove the wheels that drove the cogs that powered the Heteroptia's headquarters (Home). Guards patrolled the iron walkways above the workers. S moved unseen through the place, his body reflecting the machines' gears and circuitry, his eyes capturing the blank stares of the workers, their skin rippling with Inf.

The Deep End

…girl's hand, he leaves the bar. An arrangement. Financial. Temporal. And he thought time had been abolished and, with it, the things he thought he no longer needed. A horn blares. He has heard that before. A release of pressure. The brief sound indicating availability, travel. A man stands in his way. He pushes past, dragging the girl behind him. She pulls on his arm. For a second he is not sure who she is and then he looks into her eyes.

"Motorbike," she says in a voice that sounds as if horses' hooves were made from piano keys.

The sounds of pool balls striking, laughter, and music drifts from the bar.

The girl gets on the motorbike, gestures for him to sit behind her. He does. They move out into the traffic. He puts his hands on the girl's hips. They zigzag through the streets and between trucks. The accelerated speed of…

…surprisingly strong. Struggling for his life, gasping at air in an attempt to live. He rolls with the priest down the embankment, attempting to gain control of their momentum. He grasps at the saffron robes, nooses his arm around the man's neck. He cannot hear the waves. They keep rolling. He tries to use his bulk to stop their fall but the sand shifts and he feels it slide and crumble under his weight. What if the priest corrupts time, changes it? He wills the priest beneath him. They stop. Brushing away the sand and flies from his face, he looks at the man. The priest's eyes are closed, blood in his nostrils, on his lips. He looks up. Breathes. The sky is blue, clouds scratch around the horizon, feral dogs at a garden party. Just clouds. Just sky. Just sea. Just sand. No people. Dragonflies. Crabs. Black bees. Faint traces of the two moons. The waves restart their feathery ruffle. The noise of their demise. He looks down. Fills his mouth with saliva.

Spits into the priest's right eye.

    The man does nothing.

    He moves his face closer, intimate, bites down on the priest's nose, tastes blood and mucus, tastes sunlight and salt water, decaying fish and rotting wood. In the priest's now open eyes he can see fear, sharp, dark, the balance of humanity, his grace, tipping to the animal, instinct, the impending loss of his future fiction imperative. He grasps the man's neck, fingers tight around organs he does not know the name of, does not care, feels the man's attempts to swallow, hears the strangled gulps, the snatched breaths, feels the words build up and burst like soup bubbles in the brothy morass of the priest's spit. He looks into the priest's mouth. His discoloured teeth, a shanty town of make do and mend. From this obscenity, drip fragments of words, syllables, morphemes, all unintelligible; dribble harsh and brittle consonants, vowels of steel and lemon.

    The priest's spit stings his eyes. He presses his weight onto the priest's pinioned arms. The priest stares at his attacker. Sees nothing, not even his own reflection. The blue of them cold and distant—an ice desert he has never before imagined. The priest turns his head and vomits, a pregnant mixture of rice, chillies, garlic, and fish sauce. As soon as the semi-liquid darkens the sand, it is set upon by translucent crabs and black flies. As if in shame, the priest turns his face away from the feast. A prisoner, now, of nothing but himself. He releases his grip from the priest's throat, grabs his jaw and turns the priest's head towards him. The traces of vomit on the priest's cheeks, the flecks of vegetable matter on his lips. He leans forward and kisses the priest, pressing his tongue into the bloody mouth. Pulls out, raises a fist and punches the priest's face, cracking his left cheekbone, feels it splinter, the sky swell, the bruise immediate, sees the priest's left eye close, the other well with tears. Lifting his weight from the prone man, he flips him on his back, grips the back of the priest's neck, pushes his face into the sand, lifts the robes up and off of his shit-spattered…

...the journey to the airport. Someone was with him. Was with him. With him. Was him. Him. Someone was. Someone was him. Someone. That he was sure. No way could he have negotiated the departure board, check-in desk, immigration, security, gate number. He vaguely recalls a movie, something to do with horses, something to do with car chases, something to do with men on a planet invaded by… A meal—salad, lettuce like airmail paper, tomatoes like escape-pod boils, toenails of onions. Plastic meat, gluey gravy, eyeballs that must have been alien sprouts, the chopped tail of a lizard—carrots. Fucking bodies. Fucking toys. He doesn't think he was constrained. Not physically. No cuffs. No ties. Chemically. A pill in the morning milk. A tablet in his tea. A capsule in his coffee. A sedative. A solitary exaltation. Because of this, time falls apart. Space—restricted to the interior of the airplane—shrinks, becomes invisible—one human referent down, one to go… But then time's fucked up anyway. Chasing itself. A dog and its tail. And its mechanical hare. Or is it a rabbit. Down the whole. He remembers as a child, flying in a plane with his parents. Where are they? Looking out onto the clouds, thinking, as all children do, that they looked like snow mountains, ice cathedrals, the head of a giraffe, the hump of a camel, the breath of an arctic dragon, but also like a giant's brain riddled with tumours, infected with growths and cancers, swellings and cankers. He does not remember landing in Bangkok, nor making a transfer and taking another flight, nor travelling by boat across the strait. He does not remember. Cannot remember. But here he is. Naked within bare walls. His flesh scoured, his mind almost blank. He tries to focus on faces, familiars—friends and relatives. One image flickers into half-being—a middle-aged man, suntanned, grey hair; and others, their precision swimming in grease, women, men, children, only the grey-haired man's face strives for definition. The doctor. Doctor. What was his name? What is his name? Doctor… Doctor… Mister… And what is his name? A… B… C… D… E… No. Not Q… Not X… Not Z… K? All there is is…

The young may not remember Thule of old, under the yellow sun, its cloud-streaked sky dusted blue, its soil icy and fine, its inhabitants living in pressurized burrows and venturing up only as a rite of passage. That Thule is a long time ago, now the surface is criss-crossed with roads and dotted with cities. The burrows have become museums to Thule's history. The rite of passage is the right to live and be Thulean—to live without and with out the Heteroptia's control. S, now in the control centre, his body flickering between glass and chrome, shining with fake sunlight, reflecting back his environment, looked up into the Terran sky.

Noon Ferry

…speculates that out of the hundred or so people disembarking from the Samui-Phangan ferry, 10%—10 of them—would be suffering from some form of mental illness. Of those sunburned, suntanned, hat-wearing holidaymakers, two or three would be certifiable, potential inmates. Schizophrenics, schizoid personalities, manic-depressives, the delusionals, the criminally insane. He plays a game. Tries to pick out the could-be would-be should-be patients solely from their appearance. The teenage girl in the red bikini top, denim shorts, sandals—nymphomaniac, kleptomaniac, bulimic. The man in his twenties carrying a camouflage backpack, his belly distended by beer and burgers, a tattoo on his left calf and one on his lower back just above his khaki knee-length shorts, bare-chested, wearing a straw cowboy hat—alcoholic, manic depressive, paranoid, given to violent outbursts, nights of madness and days of suppressed regret. The middle-aged couple, both the colour of a Gucci handbag—lives of perpetual denial, narcissism—the man: victim and perpetrator of incest, rapist, domestic bully prone to verbal and physical violence; the woman: victim, secret eater of chalk and plaster, addicted to pain killers and prescription drugs, dog fondler. The institutions of madness could be limitless. An asylum containing a tenth of humanity… An asylum the size of… And he imagines that place. Blocks upon blocks, rows upon rows, tiers upon tiers of wards, of rooms, of beds. Giant wheels turning, driving the machinery—glass, and chrome, and white ceramics. The ferry empties and other passengers begin to board. He takes out his notebook and a pencil, writes…

…stares into those of the dead priest, bloodied flecks with sand and flies. He pulls himself up, backwards, rests on his elbows, and heels, feels things crawling beneath him—plastic water bottles, cans, empty cigarette packets. Clouds cover the sky, draped, rain threatens and then promises, pockmarks the sand. He stands, takes hold of the priest's robe and hauls him down the beach. At the shoreline, he pushes the body into the swell and returns to the strip of littered vegetation separating the road from the beach. There, among the fallen coconuts, palm fronds, and dead leaves, he finds discarded bricks and washed-ashore stones. He collects them and takes them down to the sea. He pushes the priest's body into the waves, the half-floating corpse compliant. The sea, shallow and clear, his partner in crime, assists him, keeps the priest buoyant, cradles him in its mass. He lets go of the body and watches it for a while, mesmerized by its rhythmic movement. A lightning flash in the distance shakes him into full consciousness and he returns to the beach to collect more rocks and bricks. Wading out to the body, he discovers small fish swimming around the priest's body. He shoos them away. He wraps the heavy objects in the priest's robes. The body sinks to the sea floor. He stands on the body, pushing it down into the sand until the body is a discarded plastic bag, a lump of rock, a new species of seaweed. He looks down. The fish return, swim over the body. A crab settles on the priest's right eye, another invades his left nostril, yet another takes residence in the swollen coral of his mouth. The accumulation of things. The order of…

…sampling the ringtone options on a mobile phone, a mynah bird goes through his range of calls—a trill, bass, ukulele, flute, wolf-whistle, car horn, trumpet. S walks with a thirst and hunger he hasn't experienced before. His mouth parched, salted spitballs drying at the corners. His guts turning somersaults, constricting, spasms of pain, muscle cramps. He walks along the shore until the low walls of the beach properties begin. Bending down by an outlet pipe, he drinks the water, tastes soap, urine, and shit. Swallows mouthful upon mouthful until he wants to vomit. Drinks until the dry riverbed of his mouth is running again with saliva. Feels the gagging muscled mass of his tongue shrink back to tongue size, the fossils of his teeth now glisten with moisture. He has no money. He scours the beach for something edible. Near the shoreline, where the small stones and shells congregate, he finds a dead fish washed up and dying in the sun. It is the colour of polished tin. Using his thumbs, he squeezes out an eye, swallows it without tasting; then the other. He takes the eyeless body back to the pipe, washes the fish, brushing away its scales, picks out the meat, chews and spits it out, drinks again from the pipe. Back at the shoreline, he sees an octopus in the breaking waves, it is purple, its head shaped like a flattened spear. He wades in after it, thrashing the water with his hands. The creature is too fast for him, flashes black and red, spurts into the depths, streamlined and perfect. Sand and pebbles suck at his feet. He struggles to free himself. Wades out. On his knees on the beach, he notices something translucent ahead of him. He crawls towards it. Crabs and flies make way, return. A jellyfish. Tendrils eaten away by fish or shrivelled in the sun. Its globular body remains, a pale limpid white with pink and blue undertones, like frozen skin or sun-flared porcelain. The centre of its body looks like the dial on an old rotary phone. Or a moulded vanilla blancmange shot with rhubarb and iodine. He digs his fingers into the mass, tears off a chunk, brings it to his mouth, bites down into it, chews, and swallows. Then on all fours, head down, biting, biting off pieces, spitting out what he cannot swallow, until the jellyfish is nothing more than a dismemberment of matter, a stage towards nothingness, a dislocation of the universe. Satiated, he stands, throws back his head, roars into the sky. Along the lengths of the beach, the dogs prick their ears, listen to the sound, somewhere between nature and all things human. The young dogs stand and run towards the noise, their hair on end but their tails wagging. The older dogs stagger to their feet, stretch, yawn, jog in the same direction. Their tongues, pink and…

The camera was the eye of a cruising vulture flying over an area of scrub, rubble and unfinished buildings on the outskirts of Bangkok. The once lush vegetation had been burned back to stubble and the river, once choked with water lilies and boats, was a dirty brown stain scarring through the soon-to-be desert. S stopped, for a second blinked back to his normality, leaned against the senso-glass, shocked by the sight of this Terran city he once knew & loved—it reminded him of his hometown Sarghyz—vibrant, electric, alive but now it was dead, dead, dead only the corporate towers of the Heteroptia HQ mimicked life.

Buddha Dogs

…younger dogs leap around the howling man, standing on their hind legs; the older form an outer circle, an honour guard of piebald, scabbed, and almost hairless dogs, some with growths on their backs, some with crippled legs—car accidents, beatings—all with scars. The man continues his roar and the younger dogs become nervous, their high-pitched barks now deeper, tinged with fear, their excited yelps turning to snarls. A large white dog, part boxer part English bull terrier, his body spotted with grey roses, walks towards the howling man. The other dogs follow. The younger dogs stop dancing, back off, crouch, raise their hackles. Who is the beachmaster? The abandoned staircase…

…cloud hangs low over the island, an upturned and suspended figure on a sarcophagus, prone, hands together in prayer, eyes closed against the waning of the light. Two heron-like birds surge in and out the surf, their serpentine necks occasionally extending into darting spears, fishing for crabs, stalking small fish, the fleeing squid. The whole world constructed, constricted, beneath the cloud, just above his nose, and he inhales the rumour of rain, feels the moisture mix with the powder-specked mucus in his nostrils, dust his eyelashes with bright and clear drops of water. Every pore of his body bejewelled with a grain of sand polished and amber, buffed and emerald. The sea. The tidal swell of his organs, the large mollusc of his liver, the sea cucumbers of his kidneys, the jellyfish of his lungs, the spiny sea urchin of his heart. And out again. Further out than ever before. His body lost to him. And then the island. And then the country. And then the continent. All of the oceans. The world. The earth. The planet—a shimmering marble, a quickly clouding eye, the continental cataracts, the North Pole's white yarmulke, the South's ill-fitting chinstrap. The racing moons of Ultima…

…is an alleyway, bricks worn down by years of urine, discarded fast-food wrappers and containers lined the sides, needless. Used condoms, always yesterday's news, that green-pink of pulped newspapers. Cold, he rubs his hands together, rubs them until they are sore, holds them to his smarting face. Above his head, a sign reads E X I T, and he shakes his head, closes his eyes, rubs the lids with his white knuckles, opens his eyes, and the sign reads B R O K E N. He looks down at the newspapers for a clue to his whereabouts, his place in the world, but the newspapers are a soggy mess; they offer no indication of time or place. He picks up a condom, tries to read the manufacturer's name, a hint of sexual geography: Jiffy, Trojan, Durex: jumps back as though from a cobra strike as a dribble of cold sperm trickles down his hand. Where is he? The condoms are unbranded, as are the needles, the crack pipes, the razor blades. A tickle and fizz of blue neon plays out at the edge of his vision. He moves towards,…

The Heteroptic Empire was falling. It was a colossal empire stretching across millions of worlds from arm-end to arm-end of the mighty multi-spiral that was the Milky Way. Its fall was colossal too—and a long one, for it had a long way to go. S was the start of that fall, the catalyst to its ultimate ruin. He would kill The Administrator, he would find the Consul, he would expose him as a charlatan, he would bring down the Heteroptia—he would set Thule free and then move out into the vast expanse of space spreading the word.

The Shallows

…above a metal door a sign reads: VSFSBRT FPHD and he pushes the door and the door opens. A man in clothing from another time, another space, ginger whiskers, a mouth lost among moustache and beard, a melting triangle of brie for a nose, eyes as intricate as shells, an overhanging brow, and above all that a stove-pipe hat, sits reading a book in a small foyer. The book cover is made of tooled green leather with gilt engravings, but the man holds the book at such an angle that S cannot see its title. There is an old writing desk and another door to the man's right. The floor is tiled in black and white rectangles becoming squares and then diamonds as S walks across it. His footsteps echo and the man tsk-tsks, disapprovingly shakes his head, slowly changing the angle at which he holds the book so that its title remains hidden to S. The second door has no handle. S knocks. The door opens. He looks into a dark hallway. A chevron of pale light shines across the floor towards the hallway's end.

"Not on my fucking planet," he hears the reading man…

…himself back out at the end of the alleyway. The street sign hazy and indistinct, the letters warping, shifting. A pink mist clouds both ends of the alleyway. The neon sign—now red—the alleyway's only form of illumination. Walls rise above him, brick upon brick, endlessly, losing themselves, losing their hypnotic solidity. He walks back to the door, looks again at the sign. It reads: CADAVER DOGS. He opens the door. There is no reading man, no desk, and the black and white tiles have been replaced by newspapers attached to the floor with packing tape. There are now five doors. Above the middle door, a sign reads: HOUSE RULES. He opens the door, the hinges, stiff with rust, creak, the bottom of the door scrapes on the floor, tearing the…

…hexagonal, has six doors. The door directly opposite S has a smaller door built within it in the bottom left-hand corner—an exact miniaturised replica of the door in which it is embedded. Six inches above the floor, in the centre of the smaller door, is a handle the size of a man's wedding ring. He watches as the door opens outward. From behind it emerges a dog. Or is it? The body is that of a Rottweiler but it has a skull for a head. The bundle of fur, muscle, and tissue that should be its docked tail is another head, which is, impossibly, growing as the beast steps into the room, its jaws snapping, saliva flying. The skull expands into the room's space becoming a crocodile's head, a horned dinosaur. He knows this cannot be happening. Even in madness, there are laws. Even in sanity there are terrible creations of pure fantasy—the hippogriff, the phoenix, the minotaur. The beast's claws shuffle-tap on the floor. Drawn to the sound, he looks down and watches as the talons turn into giant insects, their pincers clacking together and he brings his hands to his ears to muffle the sound—like a million castanets—and, as he does so, the noise stops and the creature disappears. The doors shrink in size until they are no longer visible. The floor is once again tiled, the black dissolving to a grey, the white becomes a pale blue. The room slowly fills with seawater, lifting him up to the ceiling that gives way to an azure sky. And as he breathes in the air with its faint tang of sea-eagle faeces and the ghosts of the fleeing moons, feathers of a firebird fall…

An impression already that things are getting narrower. Don't puzzle too much, S told himself. Don't turn round. Don't stop. Don't force the pace. For no visible reason, no reason. Speed had become necessary. The imminent discovery of his presence by the security guards meant that the overall plan had to be modified and hurried into execution. But without changing anything—it was too late—of the elements that made it up, and that were now inevitable. He remembered. He touched the senso glass while looking out onto the denuded city. An action of love and regret. The glass would have transmitted his dermprints to control, sampled his TDNA, they would know he was using morph-ine, they would be watching for the slightest change in the building's pattern. Time narrowed to a point where it threatened to invert and move backward, space folded, and he saw the room he will be in, saw the look of fear on the face of The Administrator.

Entertainment Complex

…white sheets, he stares at the air-conditioning unit, the blades, the primitive cousins of an airplane's ailerons, the spiracles of monstrous termites, albino fish blind and grubbing at the bottom of a sulphur-loaded ocean. A forest of cicadas, a helicopter taking off, the air-con's breath plays out over his exposed penis, gently stroking it into life. His hand glides up over his testicles, along the shaft, his thumb and forefinger gripping his tight foreskin, playing it up and over the glans, up and over until a clear drop appears and he spreads it over his cock with his right index finger, shining the bell, his hairless balls shrinking, retracting, the shaft straining violet against his shaved and roseate pubic skin that contrasts sharply with the tan of his legs, arms, and torso, as if that part of him—the organs of sex and emission—were disembodied, the severed statuary of an anaemic god dug from the earth, dredged from the sea, the genitals and buttocks the calcified remains of a once living thing. Once perfect. He looks down at his tanned hand rhythmically stroking his pale pink cock as if it were somebody else's hand, somebody else's cock, doubly removed, and again, until there is three of them, of him—penis, hand, eye. He is being masturbated, he is masturbating, he is watching himself being masturbated, he is watching himself masturbate. He looks into the mirror hanging on the wall facing him. He watches himself watching himself and he sees six, no seven, a seven-fold sex. And he is watching back, watching himself watching himself watching himself. The mirror self watching him watching the mirror self. Numbers become his only language. The 1 of the penis, the 0 of the urethra. The 00 of the testicles. The 0 of his anus. The 2s, 6s, and 9s of his scant pubic hair. Multiplying. Multiplicities. He looks into the mirror-self's eyes and sees himself replicated back. Him in his eyes. His in him. Endlessly. Then the eyes = the zeroes within zeroes, the infinity of both eyes. Golden hand against pale pink cock, golden hairs highlighted against pale brown, the crystal lubricant mixing with salty sweat, the tears in his eyes, the warp of the mirror, the shiver of his muscles, the semen warm and pooling in his navel, on his knuckle and in his palm. Raising up on both elbows, he stares again into the mirror. He notices his hair has been cropped close, the razor leaving a fine halo of blond and, for a moment, his astigmatic vision creates a double, a flickering aura. He stands, dizzy, as if he is waiting for the other to catch up, to re-inhabit him. Focusing, he opens the curtains, looks down onto the street, at the food vendors assembling their stalls, unstacking tables and chairs, firing up their calor-gas stoves; yet others selling fruit: mango, papaya, pineapple, different types of melon; yet more filling bottles with Tizer-coloured gasoline; and the road is filled with tuk-tuk drivers, moped-taxis, cabs all green and yellow, fuchsia-pink. Bangkok. He pulls the cord to close the curtains and a cockroach scuttles across the balcony, and he watches as its scent trail follows in…

…28th (March), Patient S seen leaving his hotel room at 8 a.m. dressed in dark blue T-shirt, black cotton knee-length shorts, brown flip-flops. The patient walked along Soi 2 onto Sukhumvit

Road, which—as I have previously noted—is heavy with both automobile and pedestrian traffic making surveillance difficult but not impossible. At 10 p.m. the previous evening—27th (March) after entering Patient S's room and installing visual and auditory surveillance devices while Patient S slept [drug induced—see pharmacological notes], I had earlier logged his sleep patterns and set my alarm for 6 a.m. to personally witness the patient waking. [Note to superiors/accounts—request for micro-REM unit to record patient's dream waves denied—deemed too much of a risk factor. I would like to respectfully record on file my disagreement with this decision]. According to flow charts, Sukhumvit Road had an estimated 30% increase in traffic (vehicular and human) for this time of day [see attached charts]. As far as I am aware, there were no festivals, holidays, or sporting events planned for this date, no student demonstrations or political rallies appeared on my report from Heteroptia Inf. I checked the traffic news and noted a traffic incident {A truck had collided with an elephant (calf-female) and its handler. The handler had been killed instantly. The truck driver taken to hospital in an ambulance. The elephant suffered two broken legs (front and back—right), a metre-long gash along its right flank, its food (bananas, mangoes, and cucumbers) crushed beneath the truck's tyres. A policeman called to the incident fired two shots into the elephant's skull just above and between its eyes (the second bullet killed the animal; the first ricocheted, breaking the window of a nearby convenience store)} but this occurrence alone could not have been the reason for the increase in traffic [both forms]. I observed the crowd and Patient S within the crowd. Observed them as one. Patient S an integral part of the human machine—with-others. I followed. Watched the crowd surge in a seemingly organized mass = deorganize, reorganize—living cells, a random serving of noodles, circuit boards, a sea of plankton. Patient S—the invading virus, the white phagocyte. The Administrator—the pursuing…

…The Administrator—14:10 28th (March) edited report. Location: Sukhumvit Road between

Soi 2 and Soi 4. Patient S proceeded on foot. I followed 20 yards behind as is recommended in the Heteroptia handbook Chapter 23, Part IV, Section iii. Patient S turned right into Soi 4 and stopped outside an entertainment mall. I observed him from across the street. Patient S seemed confused. He appeared [through my observation of body language] confused and unsure whether or not to enter the establishment. He remained outside for 20 minutes, occasionally accosted by beggars and people selling what looked like fake tattoos, and others selling bangles, ties, and fruit. 14:40—secondary report. Observing patient's environment. My analysis of the scene indicated a second man who had also stopped in the location for the duration of my surveillance of Patient S. The man stood at the south-east corner of Sukhumvit Road and Soi 4. The majority of the time he was looking south. Dressed in formal Western apparel, the man had the appearance of a company executive or an embassy employee [minor Thulean diplomat?]. The man's blond hair was closely cropped. I noticed that his gaze was not constant. It appeared, in fact, to be fixed on something insubstantial—he was staring at a point just above my head and beyond the limits of human…

The man in the chair was as naked as the room's bare white walls. They had shaved his head and body completely; only his eyelashes remained. Tiny adhesive pads held sensors in position at a dozen places on his scalp, on his temples close to the corners of his eyes, at each side of his mouth, on his throat, over his heart and over his solar plexus, and at every major ganglion down to his ankles. He was obese and his skin was different shades of grey as if camouflaged in shadows. The Administrator. Each ganglion was a solar system and each nerve ending a planet. The Administrator's body was the Heteroptia's Solsys command centre, was the source and means of disseminating the Inf, it sucked in the extra-Inf from the galaxy and transformed it to intra-Inf, sending it out again in a new form—Heteropticized, pure and crystallized non thought, anti-being. The Administrator controlled the planets and their inhabitants—The Heteroptia Consul controlled The Administrator. S walked towards the array of flesh and sensors fully aware that The Administrator knew he was there.

Chinese Boxes of Russian Dolls on Packets of Porridge Oats

…the smells of south-east Asia: burning meat, effluence, candy-sweet, over-ripe, car fumes, fish, talcum powder, pepper and lime, chlorine and salt, sweat and fungus. White tiles in a blue pool, two lines of black tiles, marking three areas of white under clear water reflecting the sky, blue pipes, the edge of the pool also tiled—dark brown ceramic squares the size and colour of chocolate pieces. Red poles rise into yellow, blue, and red stanchions, which, in turn, are affixed to a pale-blue ceiling. The roof candy-striped red and white, the walls of the pool bar area white with geometric patterns painted in primary colours—red circles, blue triangles, yellow squares— each chair a different colour. The sun and wind shifting the tones, the shadows, making everything ripple, elide, approximate. His eyes taking time to adjust to…

…garden area that leads to the pool bar, as if nature mirrored or mimicked the manufactured objects—the blooms of white, red, and yellow—he was sure one of the trees was a magnolia; inhabited by grey and white squirrels, it overhung the pool, occasionally letting fall a white petal, a yellow stamen, a green leaf. He didn't know the names of the other trees, did not know the species, their taxonomy, but they too let fall flowers, fruits, and petals, so that the pool became a shifting reflection of the static area surrounding it, and that area became, in turn, a reification of the liquid world. The crazy-paving wall, the stones buried…

…objects from nature and from with-out associate themselves with the overhanging light bulbs, the windblown lanterns, the leaves with the shifting squares of missing tiles on the pool floor, the offerings on the Buddhist shrine with the table full of bottles, books, laptop computers, mobile phones. He is on his knees…

The jump is instantaneous. To a photon, the whole history of a universe may be like this: over in a flash, before it's had time to blink. To a human, it's disorienting. One moment you're an hour out from the last planet you visited—then, without transition, you're an hour away from the next. But to a Thulean, the jumps were laborious, glacial. The photon's blink was the age of the earth up until the mammals appeared; the age of Thule when it ran with fresh water and sunlight. As the galaxy pulsed through The Administrator's body, as the delicate veins in his eyelids controlled the tides on Enzian 4, and the quick of his right pinky finger swept winds through the immense forests of Nargaz Prime, so S slowly approached wondering in what part of The Administrator's body he resided, in which part his slow approach was being monitored—The Administrator's right eye twitched as firestorms on S-Latje raged out of control. For the time being. For the time.

Ejector Seat

…think he was always being followed, he would think he was always being followed. He seems to have arrived here instinctively. He had no option but to turn left out of the hotel, the Baptist Church blocking his way to the right. He hates turning left. But at the top of the road he had choices: straight on, left, and he had turned right, unthinking, knowing, somehow, where to go, and that his journey would be a short one, no longer than five minutes; yet his destination was vague, a space that held a lot of people, but he was in a city, that space could be anywhere, any thing, any place. As he walked, the space became filled not only with people but with music and light, loud voices in many languages, some of which he understood, others that he had a vague knowledge of, and the rest a broken glockenspiel of fricatives, plosives, and sibilants. Transitional communications…

…traffic lights. The people stop, like a rippling sheet on a newly made bed. Under a tall tree, near a room where the walls are the colour of sorrel and salmon sauce. No letters from…

…night, just before bed, he listens to her pee (verb). "Yeh, yeh, yeh! Just a little bit. Fiddlesticks. Yeh!" it says. The sound it makes. He wishes his bodily functions were as regular. As joyous. Such a small vocabulary. Whereas, his urination is pure noise: VVVVVVRRRRRMMMMM! BBBWWWSSSHHH! VVRRRRVVVTTT! As a matter of fact, that is the meaning…

In the beginning was the cry: alarm, anguish, terror, chemically pure pain: prolonged, sustained, piercing, to the limits of the tolerable: phantom, spectre, monster from the netherworld of Thule: a disturbing intrusion at any event: disruption of the urban rhythm, of the harmonious chorus of sounds and voices of supernumeraries and beautifully dressed actors and actresses: an oneiric apparition: an insolent, brutish defiance: a strange, transgressive presence: a radical negation of the existing order. The plug pulled—the light flickered, space trembled—The Administrator blinked in and out—drawing power from the cities, the earth, the galaxy. The Inf like a runaway train, a lover slipping through closing elevator doors. A dreadful sound filled the room—the billion utterances of his name, delayed, reversed, played over, speeded up, layered——S-S-S-S-S-S-S-S-S-S-S-S-S-S-S-S-S-S-S-S-S-S-S-S-S-S-S-S-S-S-S-S-S! The last hiss of the dying. He knows. There are too many. There are not enough.

The Architecture of Shells

…the vines run large red ants. Along the vines. The veins. Within his veins run large red ants. Ants. Angst. Anti-bodies. Anti-human bodies. Is there anything insectile about the human body? Some common ancestor? Not their multi-faceted eyes. Not their antennae. Not their pincers. Wasp-waisted. Blue-ass fly. Beetle-browed. Bee-stung lips. His tongue explores his teeth, albino honeycombs each containing a single grub, raw nerves, he bites down to release them but they remain entombed. Dead. Something different…

…what brought him here. He stands outside a building. The crowd around him, of which he is surely a part [apart], quivers and rests, lunges and parries. A tonal variance in the air engages and then disengages with his thoughts, memories pirouetting around wishes, the flashback surge into the now, dislocating ideas, relocating desire. The bite and swallow of the crowd, the traffic's dodge and boil, the hush and crescendo of the Skytrain, superimposed on his language, becoming its grammar, its alphabet and dictionary, the punctuated layering of the city. There is the elementary…

…two glass doors in front of him. He cannot see through them. On each door, a brass handle, intricate, trombone-like. Below each handle a sign, one in a language he does not know, or cannot remember, arabesque letters; the other in a different but more familiar language, the letters—red on gold—twitch and convulse, then stop: Push. There is nothing…

Once upon a time when the world was young there was a Thulean named S.

Fresh Meat

…a building site, all rubble and dust, an idle crane, a resting digger, no workmen to be seen. But the place reeks of motion, penetration, the slow pivot of metal arms, the wringing of hands. Out of a powder-grey mass, out of a two-dimensional formation, a grid, of lines and angles, a collective node of contrasted spaces, each space a private theatre of intractable actions and irretractable thoughts, the pleasure and fear of…

…the bed, he looks around the room. The walls are painted a pale green. As he stares closely at the wall opposite, he notices beneath the paint a pattern of sorts, maybe old wallpaper beneath the paintwork. Focusing, he thinks he is able to discern reeds or leaves of some kind. Five-pointed, splayed. He stands. Moves closer. The pattern is repeated around the room, on all three walls. He looks up at the pink ceiling. There, too. Standing in the middle of the room, he slowly turns around trying to discern a secondary pattern, a symmetry, but can find nothing, no unifying grid. Some of the leaf shapes are side by side, some far apart from each other, yet others overlap so the leaf has ten points, fifteen, twenty, and then he realizes that these markings aren't fronds, or reeds, or leaves, they are handprints, hundreds, thousands of handprints on all three walls, on the ceiling, hands pressed into the paintwork, into the very plaster. This obscene…

…pushes her dark nipple and it gives a little like a pen top, he bends to…

Just outside the expanding light cone of the present a star died, iron-bombed. Something—some exotic force of unnatural origin, twisted a knot in space, enclosing the heart of a stellar furnace. A huge loop of superstrings twisted askew, expanding and contracting until the core of the star floated adrift in a pocket universe where the timelike dimension was rolled shut on the scale of the Planck length and another dimension—one of the closed ones, folded shut on themselves, implied by the standard model of physics—replaced it. An enormous span of time reeled past as S entombed The Administrator's testicles in the grip of his right hand. From somewhere deep within his circuits, far far away in another space-time, The Administrator stirred. Came up through the dimensions like a deep-sea diver riding up on the knotted rope of his pressure levels. S waited patiently. In this room, time was glacial, as slow as Sunday, while outside a handful of seconds ticked by.

The Trenches

…neural. Compulsive. He opens the door. The hallway is bright and cool, air-conditioning hums while fans above his head turn chopping the breeze downward, imperceptibly feathering the hair on the back of his neck. Different beats of music from the numerous bars. Flickers of light. Then the music merges. The light undulates. The air around him inflates, pressurizes; then deflates, recoils in his lungs. The people in the complex pierce and flinch in an intuitive choreography. Eyes to the ground, lips pursed, a soft shuffle of desire and release. But is this really…

…claustral margins. Flexes his fingers. Splays them. Wiggles his toes. Arches his foot. Tenses his calf muscles. Pivots his knees. Relaxes his thigh muscles. Clenches his buttocks. Retracts his testicles. Shifts his penis. Rolls his hips. Sucks in his belly. Breathes out. Breathes in. Swallows. Grinds his teeth. Sniffs. Closes his eyes. Opens them. Furrows his brow. Spreads his fingers. Scissors them. Fillets his toes. Machine-guns his foot. Machetes his calf muscles. Mangles his knees. Severs his thigh muscles. Guillotines his buttocks,. Grenades his testicles. Razors his penis. Slices his belly. Breathes fire. Breathes ice. Rattles. Pulverizes his teeth. Drowns. Corkscrews his eyes.

Spikes them. Knuckledusts his brow. Transfinite options. Always. Mirrors leading back to mirrors leading back to mirrors leading back to…

…felt the words on his tongue, so many scales of vocabulary, peel off, stick to his teeth, and then fly out into the conditioned air. The words hold no meaning for him, raw, containing blood and pus, motile scabs, dead skin; but the person who consumes them, smiles, replies and turns away, returning after a few minutes with a cold drink and a piece of paper covered in blue signs. Then inchoate, tectonic shifts in his psyche. What makes this materialist? The lapidary movement of memory…

When the universe was not so out of whack as it is today, and all the stars were lined up in their proper place, so you could easily count them from left to right, or top to bottom, and the larger and bluer ones were set apart, and the smaller, yellowing ones pushed off to the corners as bodies of a lower grade, when there was not a speck of dust to be found in outer space, nor any nebular debris—in those good old days it was the custom for consuls, once they had received their Diploma of Heteroptic Psychological Excellence to visit distant star systems to re-educate the inhabitants of distant planets as to the history, culture, and science of Terra. Now, the doctors have been assumed into one being The Heteroptia Consul—all-seeing, all-understanding, all-powerful. And The Heteroptia Consul was everywhere and nowhere, but something was happening and The Heteroptia Consul rolled over the universe like a giant wave stirred by hurricanes and volcanoes. The Administrator called to him.

The Process

…seethed, he felt as though he were underwater, objects losing their solidity, the slow movement of limbs, bodies merging with the element confining them. An accretion of layers, as if the water had turned to ice, or plates of glass, panes layered one on top of the other, so his vision became fractal, fractured, and next to him on the bed, seen as if in a museum exhibition case, its glass canopy spiderwebbed with cracks, covered in dust, is a young man, his cock darker than the rest of his body, long black pubic hair, bony hips, a taut stomach, and he sees firm and perfectly symmetrical breasts, a strong jaw, high cheekbones, thick shoulder-length hair dyed chestnut brown, and he looks down again at the cock, small, hooded, the long slim legs, painted toenails, the carapaces of exotic beetles. Sees an escape into a world…

…the spartan room he sees: a bottle of Chang beer in a cooler sleeve (Tiger brand). A small fridge, the door open, containing two bottles of water, an ice tray. On a stool—his clothes, shorts, T-shirt, no underpants. Beneath the stool, his flip-flops. On the floor by the side of the bed, a used condom full and bloodied on the outside. The person in the bed next to him rolls over, lets out a long fart. S kneels to breathe it in, brothy and sweet. Nothing. Nothing else. Nothing else in the room. In the room. Room. He feels he is falling down into himself. Collapsing in. But it does not reduce…

…variable scale between the animal and the angel in man. But who is to say at what point on the graph between the horizontal axis (x) and the vertical axis (y) man truly resides? In 1239, Pope…

Smart machines lurked about the suite, their power lights in the shuttered dimness like the small red eyes of bats. The machines crouched in niches in brilliant walls of Thai tile work: a metacomp, a wetborg, a motion-sensor. A geo-sim squawked and rattled noisily in the corner, emitting a potent reek of fish oil, chillies and excrement. S tripped the motion sensor. The Administrator already knew he was there. The electric-chrome spine of the wetborg blinked green and magenta and as if the room were a mouth, a voice came from everywhere – "I see you have found me, Thulean," the voice of the Heteroptia Consul said.

Solitary Exaltation

…erase it. Ghost. Abortion. The tiny flecks of rubber. The funeral parlour. A collection of cells. The skin of a chicken blackened on a metal grill. Sizzling fireworks of fat. Inseparable. Impermanent. Immanent. Imminent. Impenetrable. The recombinant lullaby of the clock. Tick…

…dropping below his own attention span, spiralling in the nowhere between consciousness and un-; brushing through the bead curtains of time, into the past, the steamy kitchen, the pungent smells, the net-curtained window. Or, conversely, the other way—always right, remember? Not to the "has-been-before" left. The sliding smoke-glass doors, the anaesthetically clean antechamber of the future—circular room, white walls, seamless. Seemless. No exit. Rather than linear, horizontal, isn't time vertical? Vertiginous? None of us can ever know. That much is evident. Is it the nexus of not knowing that strings it all together? Stops us falling through. The grid of ignorance. The matrix of doubt and dependency. "Do you ever know your right mind?" Right—always right. Memory—past. "He was in his right mind." If we pooled everything we all knew, everything everyone has ever known, everything that can and has ever been imagined, would that make up even a billionth part of what is There? Here? And what if we included the instincts of animals, their fears, their needs? The stalking lion. The diving kestrel. The sonar of whales. The x-ray vision of the firebird? The scent run of cockroaches. The replicating viruses. A middle-aged Thulean woman swims lazily in the pool, her skin tanned, age spots like dirty constellations on her skin. Three young girls, four, six, and eight years old, sing songs in the shallows, their voices modulated by the pool's echo and reverb, making them sound older, more worldly. Between the girls—static, then splashing, at play—and the woman—moving, fighting against time in the deep end—are millions upon millions of other women above and below the surface, gasping for air, their mouths open, black holes of mortality. A curve ball thrown by…

…mother sat at the end of the dining table spraying cream onto something red on her plate. A woman, vaguely recognizable, to his mother's right, looks sideways at him at the other end of the table. She smiles, furrows her brow, purses her lips and mouths,

"You all right?"

He looks at her for a moment, watches her features coalesce into someone he once knew. He gently nods, and mouths back,

"I'm fine. Don't worry."

And his mother says,

"OK. If you're…"

From the depths of the Heteroptia's unconscious, The Administrator heard something that called. Sharp, it broke the layers into which he had sunk, damaging his perfect state of nonself. The Thulean had escaped and made his way to the Heteroptia headquarters, had somehow evaded security and was in The Administrator's suite. The Heteroptia Consul hurtled through spacetime

Corrupt Time Corrupt Space

…reality has been chewed on, the lacy result of some LSD-ravaged mutant Huguenot beetle, barely hanging together, perforated, there is a disengagement—from others, from the human, from the world. But is a disengagement from the Real possible? A possibility. A rose is a rose is a rose is a word is a world. He looks…

…in the mirror, diffracted pixels, the face barely holding together, the eye faceted, the image…

…from the table, kisses the woman he thinks he knows on the forehead. His mother (so his memory insists) he kisses on the cheek. He opens the door. The corridor is dark. Always. The plane's landing gear unfolds like plant stems, tasting the cloud's…

Doctor Sexton looks in the mirror; staring back at him is the Heteroptia Consul. He speaks: "For many years S claimed he could remember things seen at the time of his birth: the prism temples of Tchitcherine 3, the racing moons of Ultima Thule, the sonic sunsets of the eastern hemispheres. Whenever he said so the elders would laugh at first, but then, wondering if they were not being tricked, they would look distastefully at the pallid face of the Thulean boy. Sometimes he happened to say so in the presence of Consuls or Administrators; then the elders, fearing he would be thought insane, would interrupt and tell him to go somewhere else and play. But of course he could not have remembered those things. According to the tenets of the Heteroptia, Ultima Thule does not exist— there are no temples, no moons, no sunsets.

Looking into a Room Through a Window High Up in a Building That Might Just Exist Somewhere Sometime

Pitch dark on Ultima Thule, Twin-Moon-Time, Earth, the Far East, the Kingdom of Thailand. A man rolls over on a bed, locks his fingers behind his head and sighs. The bars in front of the windows give him a clue to his whereabouts. On a small wooden table next to his bed, a telephone rings. He waits. Lets it ring a hundred times. Counts. Picks it up on the one hundred and first. Closes his eyes. Nods. Replaces the receiver. Gets out of bed. Walks across the room five paces to the door. Turns the handle. The door is locked. He clicks the light switch. Nothing happens. He crosses back to the bed. Ten paces. He picks up the receiver. Listens. Static. He says, "It's S."

Sampled Texts:

Cosmos Incorporated – Maurice G Dantec, *We Can Remember it For You Wholesale* – Philip K Dick, *Snow Crash* – Neal Stephenson, *Endymion* – Dan Simmons, *The Gateway Trip* – Frederik Pohl, *Warlord of Mars* – Edgar Rice Burroughs, *Neuromancer* – William Gibson, *Behold the Man* – Michael Moorcock, *The Idyll* – Maurice Blanchot, *Gravity's Rainbow* – Thomas Pynchon, *Schismatrix* – Bruce Sterling, *Matter* – Iain M Banks, *Moving Mars* – Greg Bear, *The Wild Boys* – William S Burroughs, *Foundation and Empire* – Isaac Asimov, *Recollections of the Golden Temple* – Alain Robbe-Grillet, *Shockwave Rider* – John Brunner, *Engine City* – Ken McLeod, *Makbara* – Juan Goytisolo, *Stranger in a Strange Land* – Robert A Heinlein, *Iron Sunrise* – Charles Stross, *The Cyberiad* – Stanislaw Lem, *Heavy Weather* – Bruce Sterling, *Confessions of a Mask* – Yukio Mishima, *Mobile* – Michel Butor, *Madness & Civilization* – Michel Foucault, *The Divided Self* – RD Laing, *Artaud Anthology* – Antonin Artaud.

THE BEAUTIFUL FIGHT

BY
MELISSA MANN

beatthedust press

Chapter A

As of this minute, I've no past. Karen Backhouse has no history, I've decided. Before this, there was nothing. I was born here just now, outside Shipley Baths, to no parents. The dawn, it was the dawn what give birth to me. From now on, any nosey bugger asks, me mother's name is Dawn. I look up and feel her hands holding me face, me new face, and I smile.

There's no one about at this time. S'like it is of a night. S'how I like it though, me. No one about. Prefer me own company to other folk's. Things allus get messy round other folk. I get messy. Nah, s'not for me. Not good for me I reckon. I like the light though. Forgot how nice it feels on yer skin an' that. When I touch me breasts or me belly or me thigh, s'like touching the light. Like I've been painted in light. Oh eh, look, there's a bruise on me leg what looks like a face. Hope it's not Jesus cos I can do without coach loads o'nutters turning up to see the miracle on me leg.

Yeah, forgot that about the light. How nice it feels. Wait, no, I never. I couldn't have forgot, could I, cos I've only just been born. 'ere just now, outside Shipley Baths. 'ere, round the back near ASDA car park. Or A DA cos the sign's broke, in't it. Wonder how long it's been like that then. Must've happened while I was off on me trip away. Yeah, must have got broke while I was off in Romania.

Seems like donkey's year since I were last 'ere cleaning. It'd've been of a night though, so I'd definitely have noticed if the 'S' were broke. Sod it! I've no past. There was no trip away cos Karen Backhouse has no history. The past belongs to other folk. S'for other folk to say, not me. I belong to now. The 'ere an' now. See, there I am in Shipley Baths' winders. S'got reflective glass to stop the pervs looking in on the women an' kiddies having a swim. S'old now though, reflective stuff's all cracked an' peeling off in bits. S'funny seeing yerself like you're on the other side o'the glass looking out. Perfect though I am, not all cracked an' peeling off in bits. Me face feels endless, like it's got no edges. I look like someone I've known all along.

Sun's gone in. Come over all cold I have now. Best get dressed before I catch me death. Catching yer death. Funny turn o'phrase that, in't it. Like death's this solid thing yer can hold in yer hands. Funny an' all, putting yer clothes back on when you've been without 'em for a bit. S'like climbing back in yer body. Bra, pants, socks, jeans, sweatshirt - like flesh almost, limbs even.

Someone's phoning me. Can feel 'em vibrating in me fist. S'her, I just know it. The past calling me. Well I'll not answer, I'll not! Stopped. Am holding me breath. Waiting. Waiting to see if the past's left us a message. I'm squeezing the phone between me palms, wringing out the past till it cuts into me. Till the cutting into me hurts. I like it though, the hurting. Pain, that special place.

Text's just come. Phone's in me left hand now. Me cutting hand. Why I think this I don't know. S'her. The text. I know like I know about me cutting hand. Instinct, must be. Yeah, instinct. I watch me fingers unfurl and there she is, screaming her name at me from the screen. JUDE. Allus shouting Jude is, mouthing off. And now am torn. Torn between lobbing the phone at the wall and pressing 'View'. Torn between the past and the present; trapped between 'em in this tiny pocket of non-time.

u cant do this 2 me u bitch i wont fuckin let u!!!!!

Things allus get messy round other folk. I get messy. Am scratching. S'the clothes. Too much on me skin, suddenly. Don't like being touched, me. Delete. S'it. Just me now. Me and the present. Phone's off. S'in me rucksack 'long with all the other crap I lug about but don't need any more – make-up bag, detachable hood, mirrors, hairbrush, knife, tape. Just crap really. I look down at me bag and give it a good kick.

"Oi, blondie!"

Sod it. Big bald bloke. I struggle into me trainers and hang the bag off me shoulder. He's heading right for me, past the trolley park. Holding his balls through the pockets of a navy Umbro coat.

"Been watching you, I 'ave," he says. Playful, sing-song voice. Grinning, he nods his head at two CCTV cameras. One on the wall o' Shipley Baths, other on the office block opposite. Sod it! "That were some show you put on fo' us," he shouts, running a hand through the idea of his hair. "'ow much I owe yer then, love? Fo' me little striptease?"

The present slows down as the bald bloke walks the last few steps towards me… the word *Security* embroidered on his breast pocket… the birthmark on his chin like a splash of Ribena… his grin fading as he clocks me face. He looks away down the slope, hand wiping his mouth, then turns back round. On his face, a smile some autistic kid has scribbled there with a crayon.

"I should…" he says to the space over me left shoulder. His Adam's apple lifts, drops. "Best get back, eh?" he says, thumbing the air by his ear.

"Eighty quid you owe me!" I shout after him. Cold words that creep down his collar, seep between his shoulder blades. I watch his neck disappear in the meat of his back. "Eighty quid, yeah! Call it a oner an' I'll throw in a quick grope. Y'up for that then, are yer? Cheeky snog an' a bit of a tit grope?" He's down the bottom now. "Oi, am soddin' talking to you, fella!" I watch him walk past the ticket machines. "Take that as a no then, shall I?" Can't see him now; he's gone round the corner. "Ah well, sod yer then. Save meself for Simon Cowell instead, the sexy beast."

I grip the strap o'me rucksack, chew on me lip. Messy being round other folk. Nah, s'not for me. S'not good for me I reckon. I like the light though. How it feels on your skin an' that. Sun's come out again. I look up and feel her hands holding me face, me new face, and I smile. Yeah, I love yer too, Mam.

Chapter B

According to the clock on Shipley town street, it was five past nine at night. As far as Karen was concerned, the clock only told four hours' worth of time a day, from 9pm to midnight. She was standing in the doorway of what used to be Woolworths, peering through the security grill. All she could see was the pic 'n' mix display in the middle of the shop floor, naked but for the odd plastic scoop. From the age of two, Karen would come to Woolies every Saturday to buy sweets with her pocket money. She looked down at her hands, remembering the feel of the paper bag and her Gran's arthritic grip. In the doorway, a copy of Shipley Target scuffled with the wind round her feet. Karen looked out across the town street. Empty shops like missing teeth in a forced smile. The metal frames of market stalls, skeletons exhumed from the concrete of the square.

"Dying on its feet, this place is," she muttered, pulling her hood up.

The arms of Shipley clock flatlining at nine-fifteen told her she should have been at work by now. If she was unlucky and the supervisor decided to check up on her tonight, Karen would be in trouble. She couldn't afford to lose her job, not in a recession. Not with unemployment in Bradford going through the roof. People were desperate for work, even night-shift jobs cleaning. Karen picked up her rucksack. A gaggle of girls in high heels and higher skirts tottered past, raucous laughter slashing the cold air like knives.

"Catch their death, they will," thought Karen, fiddling with her coat zip. "Barely an outfit between 'em." She looked at their Thursday-night-out-after-work faces - fierce blusher, fuck-me lipstick, glitter eyeshadow. In Karen's rucksack, the mirrors, make-up bag, hairbrush, knife and tape. Sirens calling to her. Not now though, not here. Barely half an hour since the last time she'd checked herself. Best wait till she got to the Baths. Karen pinched the hood under her chin, and headed off down the high street.

*

Karen, hiding on the floor behind the counter. Beside her, a mop, bucket and a roll of bin liners. On the other side of the meeting room, two women having an argument. Karen had just started cleaning up after the local women's group, when the pair burst back in. Karen listened, eyes fixed on the plastic stomachs spilling out the fist-holes punched in a row of crisp boxes.

Jude Boyd thumped her black cowboy boot on the seat of a plastic chair. A tall, hefty woman, her hair steel grey, twisted into dreadlocks and drawn together like kindling with a bootlace. A silver stud in her left nostril unashamedly drew attention to a large hooked nose. Her eyes, the colour of violets and etched with black kohl, swept the meeting room fiercely.

"Ten fuckin' people, Yve. You told me there'd be forty. At *least* forty you said!" She jabbed her finger at the other woman. Yve nervously pushed the round, tinted glasses up her nose. Her other hand gripped a table strewn with flyers and booklets.

"Jude, I don't know what to say…" Yve began, folding her arms. "I was told… the chair of the Baildon & Shipley Women's Group led me to believe…"

"Baildon an' Shipley Women's Group. Jesus Christ! Why the fuck am I wasting my time wi' these people any road?" said Jude, batting the air with her hand impatiently. "Why the hell I let you talk me into this gig, I don't know. Am worth more than this, Yve, you know that. It's not s'long back I was packing out St George's Hall."

"Once, in '97, warming up for Pam Ayres," muttered Yve, rearranging her skirt. The tiny bells on the hem tinkled irritably.

"Not that you'd know based on tonight's bloody fiasco," Jude continued, pushing the chair away with her boot. "Now I can't even fill a meeting room at Shipley Baths, apparently." Jude kicked over a waste bin, scattering plastic cups across the blistered linoleum.

"Shit!" Ignoring the brown liquid leaking towards her foot, Jude pulled Jesus from her cleavage and stabbed the cross into her lip. "What a bloody mess."

Yve headed across the room in search of a cloth, her fleece-lined Crocs stubbing out a trail of rubber mice on the floor. "Oh!" she said suddenly, clutching the V of her cardigan. "I'm sorry, I'd no idea…"

"Am jus'… I were jus'… cleaning up," said the back of Karen's head. She pushed up the sleeves of her fleece nervously. A spitting sound, then a pink Marigold rubbing circles in the floor with a J-Cloth.

"What the fuckin' 'ell you creeping about down there fo', woman?" said Jude, looming over the counter. "Spying on us, are yer? You from that mob in Leeds, what keep nicking me material?"

"Of course she's not spying on us, Jude," said Yve, spreading her arms to indicate the mess in the meeting room. "She's here to clean up. She's the cleaner."

"Well, she'll not get much cleaned lurking about down there, will she," said Jude, lifting the collar of her black leather coat. "Stand up, woman. Are yer' ashamed or what?" she added, rearranging her dreads. "Listen, there's no shame in cleaning; honour in cleaning. Stand up I said, cos there's no fuckin' honour creeping about on't floor, that's for sure! Jesus, this is what we're up against, Yve. Two thousand an' bloody nine an' we've still got women down on their hands an' knees scrubbing floors with their dignity!"

Karen looked down at the legs that had stood her up. She was wedged in the corner at the back of the counter, cleaning products pressed to her chest. "P-personality in cleaning… I… I reckon, anyway," she said, making a life's work out of one sentence. "Cleaning products, they've got, like charisma, an't they – Flash, Lime Lite, Cillit Bang. Sound like tranny acts from one o' them clubs off Manningham Lane."

"What's she saying, Yve. I can't hardly hear 'er. Speak up, lass if yer've got sommat to say," Jude picked up a leaflet from the counter. "What *you* need is this."

Karen kept her eyes fixed on the floor and bit her lip.

"Oi, lady, I'm talking to yer!" said Jude, flapping the leaflet violently. Karen dropped the roll of dustbin liners. Blinking rapidly, she watched it flick-book to a stop next to a mouse-trap.

"Leave her be, Jude, you're making her uncomfortable," said Yve, gripping the edge of the counter. "She's not interested."

"Don't be daft, of course she's interested. How can any woman in her right mind, not be interested?" Jude slapped the front of the leaflet. "'ere then, teck it."

Karen pulled off her rubber glove and reached for the piece of paper. Jude wouldn't let go. Her fingers gripped the sheet, eyes locked on the track marks on Karen's forearm.

"Cat… kitten," said Karen, pulling her sleeves down. "Scratched me… I were playing with it an'…

"Yeah," said Jude, nodding, violet eyes fixed on Karen's. "Nasty fuckers, cats."

Karen turned her back and busied herself rearranging the perfectly stacked boxes of Seabrook Crisps on the shelf. Beefy, cheese and onion, pickled onion, sea salt and black pepper, tomato ketchup.

"Come on Yve, let's get usselves off," said Jude, lining up the silver gargoyle rings on her left hand. "Things to do, places to be, remember? We've wasted enough bloody time with the so-called women of Baildon an' Shipley. A lost fuckin' cause, the lot of 'em, you ask me.

The flap of Jude's leather coat, bells tinkling in its wake, then the meeting room door catching in the frame. Karen waited, listening for evidence of a return. Nothing. Just air and water in an old radiator knocking to come in. Karen looked at the counter. Amidst the paper plates of custard creams and half-eaten cheese sandwiches, the leaflet.

RECLAIM THE CUNT, REGAIN THE FEMININE! – A Seminar on Female Beauty led by renowned Feminist-Anarchist, JUDE BOYD.

Karen folded the sheet in two and slipped it in her pocket. Then, grabbing her rucksack from under the counter, she fled the meeting room for the ladies' loo.

*

Karen was kneeling on the toilet lid in front of the mirror. On the cistern, her make-up bag and hairbrush. The light in the ladies room plinked intermittently overhead. Karen looked at her face and saw lies. Not the smooth white skin flushed pink from her hasty dash downstairs, but lines. Lines where there shouldn't be lines. Folds of skin where there shouldn't be folds. Flaws, everywhere flaws. It was like someone came into her room while she slept and added things to her face they knew she'd hate. A weird kind of stealing. Karen eyed her profile critically. Pressed down on the end of her nose. Pulled at the skin round her eyes.

Stuck to the ledge above the cistern, bits of wig tape. Karen was sticking them to her face, fixing her skin where she felt it needed to go. Fifteen minutes later, she confronted the mirror and stared at her reflection. Stared until she was the only person left in the world.

"Perfect," she said eventually, nodding at the deformed lie of herself. Then, frowning, she leaned in closer and fingered the mole on her chin.

"Karen?" The cleaning supervisor.

Karen pulled her Gran's watch, an old Casio with a silver link strap, from the pocket of her jeans. 22:21.

"Sod it," she whispered, hands dithering between face, make-up bag and the rucksack wedged in the sink. "Am… am in 'ere, Mrs Ramsden, cleaning the bogs… toilets," she called, wincing as she ripped the bits of tape off her face. "… be out in a sec," she added, struggling to get the sticky tabs off her fingers.

"You an' I need to 'ave words, Karen Backhouse."

Karen brushed her hair into two sheets of pale electricity, then opened the toilet door.

"The meeting room on the first… oh good God in 'eaven," said the supervisor, stepping back. "Whatever's the matter with yer…?" she asked, pointing uncertainly at Karen's blotchy face. Karen's breath reversed down her throat. "Have you got eczema or…?"

"What? Oh… oh no, it's not… it's…," Karen said, looking at the floor, "…I think am allergic to that new cleaning stuff wot we're having to use. Must've had some on me glove an' touched me face with it or sommat. It's… it's nowt, really." Karen headed for the door. "Best get on, eh. A right pig 'ole it is upstairs after that women's meeting. Tried to make a start on it before, but then two of 'em came back an' I'd to knock off."

"Yes, yer better 'ad get on, an' sharpish," said the supervisor, consulting the watch lashed to her forearm. "Five and twenty past ten, it is now." Karen didn't wait to hear any more. "And think on when yer use that cleaning spray in future," the supervisor called after her. "Cos yer've made a right bloody mess o' yer face. You want to watch yerself, you do, Karen, else yer'll do yerself a damage."

Chapter C

Used to bring Gran 'ere in her wheelchair when she got old. Could sit 'ere for hours, she could - hours what passed like shaggy dog stories. Yeah, loved Robert's Park, Gran did. She'd not like it now though. Gone to the dogs now. Turn in her grave if she saw what they've done to the shelter. Used to sit in there to eat us chips. Burnt out shell, it is now. And the graffiti! I look up at the sign what the council's stuck on the shelter wall. *Keep Out. No Trespassing.* Underneath some joker's written *yeah, like you'd fucking want to* in red marker pen. School kids from Salt's I reckon. Used to see 'em hanging round 'ere of a lunchtime, smoking an' that, having a go at folk walking their dogs. It'll've been one o' them. Messing about, trying to set fire to their farts for a laugh.

No, she'd not like it 'ere now. Turn in her grave if she saw what they'd done to us shelter. Only thing what eats in there now is vermin. I could just eat a bag o' chips, thinking about it. Come over all peckish all of a sudden. S'not gone nine yet though. They'll not be open till noon I reckon, earliest. Still, I'll have a wander over, see what time they start frying. Can allus come back later. I shoulder me rucksack and feel me face smile. Feel it move before it does it sometimes. S'funny that. Like feeling's a thought as well as a sensation.

I were right, noon. Ah well, can allus come back later. Or I could make me own. End Shop's open. I could go in there, get some spuds. Yeah, I'll make me own. Not the same off a plate, mind, but still.

I've forgot what I've come 'ere for now. S'the problem when you've no past, there's nowhere for old thoughts to go. Nowhere for 'em to stay. Yeah, Karen Backhouse has no history. I forgot that earlier, at the shelter. I've remembered now though. Just now when I saw them morning papers in the shop winder. Reminded me why not having a past is important.

I've forgot what I've come 'ere for now. It wan't for them though. Din't come 'ere for them - the *Daily Mirror* or *The Sun* or the *Guardian* or the *Yorkshire* soddin' *Post*.

BAILED BOYD – THE MOST HATED WOMAN IN BRITAIN?

WHAT A CULT!

FEMINIST ACTIVIST DENIES GBH

BOYD'S HOME BESIEGED BY ANGRY MOB

No, I din't come 'ere for them. S'the past calling me. The past wearing dark glasses and giving the Vs through the side winder of a Nissan Micra. Well I'll not look, I'll not! An' I'll not go in the shop now, neither.

"Why yer crying, lady? Is it cos you is sad?"

There's a kid stood next to me outside the End Shop. Asian he is, about six. He's wearing pyjamas, bright blue with a Thomas the Tank Engine motif. The bottoms he's got tucked in a pair of ankle-length wellies. They're green, frog's eyes staring out the toes.

"No, I ain't sad," I say, wiping me eyes on me sleeve. "Where'd you spring from then, anyway. Nearly fell out me soddin' pants, yer daft sod." In the shop winder, the past staring up at me. I'll not look, I'll not!

"From in there, in't it," says the kid, pointing at the shop door. "We own't paki shop. Well, me Dad does. That's us bedroom up there." He picks a plastic dinosaur off the pavement and holds it up. "Jamila just dropped it out winder, din't she."

"Why'd she do that, then?" I ask, looking up. Wet drips back round me ears.

"Cos she's a bloody shit, in't it," says the boy, galloping the brontosaurus along the winder ledge. "I've sorted her now though, yeah. Lamped her one with me other sister, Shazia's hair straighteners. She'll not do it again." The boy's stood right in front o'me now, running his finger along the dinosaur's spikes. "Is you crying about yer face? Is that why you is sad?" He's looking straight at me now. S'like he's pissing in me eyes. I turn away, feeling me face frown before it does it.

"Was you in a car crash?" The boy looks inside the cave of his hands where the dinosaur's hiding. "Or did some mad man come at yer with a knife, like?"

I press a hand to me cheek then tug on me fringe. "Mind yer own business, yer nosey bugger!" I say, burning a hole in the crown of his head. "I'll give yer car crash, yer cheeky sod."

"I were only askin', lady." The boy is folding the toy in the hem of his pyjama top.

I've got me purse out now. "'ere, hold yer hand out," I say, glancing briefly at the shop winder. He sticks out his mitt. Muck caught in the lines of his palms has crocheted a lace glove on his hand. I start counting the brass out. One, two, five, six quid in various denominations of shrapnel. "Right you, go inside, sam all them papers together, then go give yer Dad what he's owed."

The kid's watching me shove the papers he's brought, into me rucksack. Hanging from his mouth, a length of ice pop - an orange tongue frozen in perpetual longing. I put the change away then pocket me purse.

"Where's me money for going, then?" says the kid, sticking out his bottom lip. It's livid orange, like the rest of his gob. In his left hand, the ice-pop slashing piss streaks on the paving stones.

"In me sod-off purse!" I say, then set off back towards Robert's Park.

"You face-ache freak show bloody shit!" the boy shouts. Then the clanging sound of the shop door bell.

Chapter D

Karen had run down the side alley the minute she saw them. Jolly's nightclub, spilling its guts of revellers all over Shipley town street like road kill. Most were pissed, thanks to a Tetley's Smoothflow keg ale promotion. Karen felt their shouts and laughter crowding in on her. Felt the noise squeezing her throat and filling her nostrils. On the street, nothing but other people, whole countries of them. Above her, the black night, mean and roofless. At the far end of the alley, she could see a light. Scraping her fingers along the brick wall, Karen made her way towards it.

It was not what she was expecting, the light. It wasn't from a streetlamp at all, but a bright neon sign. A huge arrow like white lightening pointing down a flight of stairs. Karen gripped the rusty banister framing the stairwell, and peered into the basement. Despite her frailty, the balustrade groaned, shifted. The steps were worn, the stone soft in the middle from centuries of shoes and boots traipsing up and down them. At the bottom, a glass showcase with a poster inside. Karen pulled on the straps of her rucksack and looked back the way she'd come. Empty. Just the metallic rings of Shipley clock chiming the half hour. '11.30,' Karen thought and bit her lip, looking the other way down the alley.

"Sod it," she said eventually, then began to edge her way down the steps.

Karen stared at the poster for The Candy Club, absently fingering her fringe. *COME AND HAVE A GO IF YOU THINK YOU'RE NOT HARD ENOUGH!* it said, then various photographs of half-naked women swirling round a metal pole. Karen stepped back from the glass case and wiped under her nose. She could smell damp. Damp that was almost medieval. The door to the left of the poster was trying to be a wall – no handle, no key hole, just an expanse of dense grey steel with hinges at one end. Karen looked at the poster again, taking in the glossy sheen on the girls' thighs, the muscle tone in their arms, their small, pert breasts.

"Na lass, you comin' in or wha'?" A female voice. Crackling, then a throat clearing itself.

Karen backed up against the wall behind her, looking up, down, left, right, like a panicked pigeon.

"Top left, love, by't air vent," said the voice, statically. "Smile, you're on Candy's camera - ha!" Then coughing like a volley of machine gun fire. Karen looked up and saw a small spherical camera eyeballing her, the green light in the centre like an anti-pupil. Feeling the blood rise in her face, Karen pulled up her hood and looked at her trainers.

"You comin' in then, love?" More coughing. "Or shall I tell security there's a junkie 'angin' round us front door lookin' to shoot up?"

"I'm not a… I'll… I want to come in," said Karen, looking up at the eyeball and pointing at the door. A buzzing noise, then a click. The steel door released itself from the frame, then opened like a slow, electronic swoon.

The female voice was sitting inside a smoke-filled booth, wearing a badly fitting wig and a flouncy pink blouse, cut low to reveal what looked like a rack of lamb.

"Am guessin' you an't been 'ere before," said the woman, sucking on a thin cigar. She held it horizontally between fingers and thumb, the nails of which had been extended to twice their length with airbrushed acrylic.

Karen nodded, then shook her head, eyes fixed on the red lipstick trapped in the thread-like crevasses feeding off the woman's mouth.

"S'free to gerrin, but yer've to pay for't dances. An' yer drinks o'course. S'a fiver a pint. Lasses what do't dances come round wi' a pint glass before they go on't stage. That's 'ow yer pay 'em. Quid if yer a tight wad, tenner if yer feelin' flush." A cough rattled inside the woman's blouse, then erupted out her mouth. She pressed her cigar-holding hand to the creped skin of her neck, and wafted the other ineffectually round her face. "No touchin', no obscenities, no drugs, an' no gerrin' rat-arsed pissed neither, else the bouncers'll be onto yer, arright? S'through there." She jabbed her cigar in the direction of a red velvet curtain. Ash tumbled down her blouse and over the Argos catalogue laid out in front of her.

Karen stood before the curtain, convinced her insecurity tag would set the alarm off as soon as she walked through it. "Go on then, in yer go," said the woman, blowing the ash off a page of curling tongs. "They'll not bite… well they will, but they'll charge yer for'it. Ha — bloody will an' all!" The woman flicked over the page then leaned in close, shutting one eye to read it.

It was brighter in the club than Karen was expecting. A Victorian chandelier cast a burnt yellow light over the bar area to her right. Small lamps, shades shaped like old-fashioned corsets, were positioned at regular intervals on the ledge that ran round the walls. The darkest part of the room was to the left of the stage. It was also the emptiest part. Most of the punters, about sixty of them, mostly men, were congregated in front of the stage. Here, a metal pole fixed to wooden floorboards, glinted suggestively in a shaft of dusty pink light.

Karen unzipped her anorak then did it up again. Even standing there in the shadows, she felt exposed. A drink would steady her nerves, give her something to do with her hands, but she couldn't face the bar. Too many people trying to get served. Just the one barman, red-faced and sweating, trying to serve them. Remembering the can of coke she'd nicked from the meeting room at the Baths, Karen took off her rucksack and knelt down to open it.

"Aye aye, good timing that." The toe of a red stiletto nudged the rucksack provocatively. "Allus know when folk're getting there brass out. I 'ave, like this sixth sense. Alarm goes off in me 'ead, an' am across the room before yer can say American Express!" A woman in a red lace thong and matching padded-plunge bra, was standing over Karen, her body as smooth and voluptuous as hope. Grinning, she jiggled her pint glass. It was barely a quarter-full. Change mostly and a note that looked foreign. "Come on then, girl, let's see the colour o'yer money. Don't normally take brass off women, but am bloody skint, to be honest. An't even worked off me fee or me taxi fare yet. I'm Angel by the way. I were born Angela, mind, which is fine if yer work in't Co-op, in't it, but not much cop if yer get yer fanny out for a livin'." She plucked a pound coin from the pint glass, tossed it up and caught it in her cleavage. "Still the same daily grind though, in't it, when yer think about it – ha ha!"

Angel drew a length of gum from her mouth and twirled it round the end of her finger, watching as Karen started pulling stuff out of her bag.

"Good God al-bloody-mighty, 'ow much stuff yer gorrin there, then?" said Angel, biting the gum off her finger end.

Karen got to her feet, rummaging in her purse. She eyed the coins in the pint glass. They looked like the taste in her mouth. "I've only… is… 'ave yer got change for a twenty? S'real an' that. Just gorrit out the cash point."

"'ave I eckers like got change, yer daft cow. I'll be lucky if there's eight quid in 'ere," said the woman, jingling her pint glass again. "I could do yer a dance for twenty squid after though, if yer want. Private, like. When am done on stage." She smiled seductively. "Thirty quid an' I'll sup from the furry cup if yer want. I don't mind. We do get the odd coach trip in from Lesbos – ha ha! Reckon there's a few in tonight, come to think of it." Angel played with her bra strap. "Anyway, look, I *like* yer; you're all right. Skinny bugger, but still…"

"Oi, I might not have your body an' that, but am no waste o'space neither. Three 'A' levels, me," said Karen, pouting.

"Yeah well, since when did 38FF brains do a lass any good, eh?" Angel pushed out her chest. "So, a dirty thirty special after then - you up for it or wha'?"

"Umm, well I don't really know… mebbe…," said Karen, playing with the toggle on her hood.

The opening beats of Sade's *Smooth Operator*.

"Shit, am on," Angel said, disappearing through the black curtain behind Karen.

"Sup from the furry cup?" muttered Karen, putting away her purse. "What the 'ell's that when it's at 'ome?"

The lights in the bar area dimmed. In the middle of the stage, the metal pole gleamed as if emitting its own light. Karen watched as the crowd pressed forward. Angel, feline and feral, slinked on stage. Shrill whistles squeezed through clenched lips as she drew an S with her back down the length of the pole. Squatting, legs apart, thighs shocking in ripped fishnets, she unhooked the front of her bra and tossed it over one shoulder. The audience cheered, the clapping like an exploding pulse. Angel cupped each breast seductively, then pushed them together, licking her lips. Karen crept towards the edge of the shadows, the swirl of body round pole mesmerising.

"Off off off off off," bayed the crowd, fists and flared hands reaching towards Angel. Leg raised, she hooked it round the pole and slowly arched her back, arms and flames of red hair licking the stage.

Karen swallowed, looking from Angel to an audience, restless and hungry. Karen's tongue felt like cardboard in her mouth. She looked around for the security guards. No one. No neckless hunks of flesh standing by. Not one man in the whole room ready to run to Angel's aid should she need it.

Legs either side of the pole, Angel bent and stretched, hands sliding up and down the metal shaft. Then, coquettishly, she hooked her thumbs through the side strings of her red thong, and pulled. The lace fell away like a cobweb. She twirled it in her fingers, then let it go. Wolf whistles, lewd shouts. Angel circled the pole, as naked and vulnerable as a little girl with her shaved crotch. Only the red stilettos gave her any sense of authority. Karen gnawed the inside of her cheek, hands balled into fists in her coat pockets. Gripping the pole, Angel lifted herself up and wrapped her torso around it. Then, very slowly, she unfurled her legs like a flower, revealing her crotch to the lustful gaze of the crowd.

"Oi, you fuckin' blind or wha'?" A woman's voice - loud, insistent.

Karen recognised Jude Boyd instantly. She had appeared from the shadows on the other side of the stage. Dreads unleashed from the bootlace, her ringed fist punched the arm of a suited man in the front row, who was trying to finger Angel's crotch.

"It says no touchin'!" said Jude, pointing at a sign on the wall. Her nose was inches from the man's sweating face.

"Yeah? And?" he said, pushing her away with the flat of his hand. "'ho the fuck are you, telling me what I can an' can't do?" Jude stared with disdain at the ghost of his hand on her shoulder.

"'ho am I?" Jude said eventually, hands on hips. "I'll tell yer 'ho I am, mate. I'm yer worst fuckin' nightmare, that's 'ho I am," she said, jabbing her finger at him. "I'm yer mother stood 'ere next to yer in this den of iniquity. Yer mother, shaking her 'ead an' wonderin' what the bloody 'ell a son of 'ers is doin' in a shit-hole like this." Jude swept her arm round the room. "A shit-hole what abuses women and turns 'em into products of mass consumption."

The man ran a finger round the neck of his collar and loosened his tie.

"Yeah, yer recognise me *now*, don't yer, yer twat. I'm the moral fibre you are sorely lacking." Jude gestured at Yve, who stepped forward and helped her up onto the stage.

"Here y'are, love," said Jude, taking off her leather coat and handing it to Angel. With the sleeves past her fingertips and the hemline touching the floor, Angel looked even more child-like.

Karen stepped back into the shadows, eyes fixed on Jude.

"'ere's a few home truths for all you so-called men out there," said Jude, tossing her dreads over one shoulder. "This place is an affront to the integrity of women, women who, at the end't day, are no different from the wives and girlfriends, sisters and daughters yer've all got waitin' fo' yer at 'ome. Women no different to yer own mothers, who, God 'elp 'em, had the misfortune to give birth to yer." Jude was shouting, trying to make herself heard over the music. She looked fiercely at Yve and pointed off stage.

"Living pornography, that's what pole-dancing is," Jude continued, eyes sweeping the room. The music stopped abruptly. Yve re-appeared giving Jude the thumbs-up. "Pole-dancing is for the poor, the abused and the hopeless. It demeans women and makes 'em victims. You lot out there, waving yer dirty money at 'em, are consumers of live human beings. It's like fuckin' cock fightin', this is, only yer've taught 'em to dance fo' yer." Jude cast her eyes along the front row. "An' speakin' o' cocks, I bet there's not one in this room what bloody works! That's why yer come 'ere, in't it, be honest. Yer come in 'ere, wavin' yer brass at some lass who as none, so yer can feel like a big swinging dick fo' once in your sorry bloody lives. It's pathetic!"

Karen watched as a hefty bloke, denim jacket over a grey hoodie, shouldered his way on stage.

"Oi, get your bloody hands off me," Jude spat at him. "Where the fuck were you, before, eh? Where were you when that poor lass needed yer to do yer job?" Jude pointed at the space where Angel had been standing. "Where were yer when that dickhead, there, was trying to prove his manhood by fingering her fanny? No-fuckin-where, mate, that's where. End of. So spare me yer jobs-worth shite, cos am norr'interested. An' I *am* gonna finish wharr'I come 'ere to say, arright?"

The security guard shaded his eyes with his hand, then gestured to someone at the back of the club. Jude continued her speech.

"Women don't exist for your sexual gratification, yeah. Women were not put 'ere on earth for men to dominate. An' they weren't put 'ere for men to buy neither. Women… I said get yer fuckin' hands off me, I mean it!" said Jude struggling in the security guard's grip. One of his colleagues grabbed her other arm. "Pole-dancing is commercial sexploitation!" Jude shouted, digging her heels in as they tried to drag her away.

Karen picked up her rucksack and gingerly backed towards the door. The security guards pushed Jude towards the wings. "It's time for women to rise up. Rise up and reclaim the cunt!" she shouted over her shoulder. From the crowd, jeers, laughter, cheering. "RECLAIM THE CUNT, REGAIN THE FEMININE!" she screamed, then disappeared off-stage.

Chapter E

Don't come in 'ere much now, not if I can help it. Just pass through. S'more a corridor than a room, really. Still think of it as Gran's though. Or the past's room, someone else's past. Spent the last eight year of her life stuck in 'ere. Funny, still smells of her, even though she's been dead forever. Rosewater, disinfectant and old hair left to clean itself. Thought I saw her in 'ere not so long back, her ghost. But it was just I-miss-you taking form. Filthy, the room is. Should run a duster round, but I can't face it.

Happy as Larry, she was in 'ere though. Wan't that bothered about going out, really. Din't like folk staring at her, what with her back all deformed and her built-up shoe. Were a blessing really when we'd to get the wheelchair. Wan't so obvious what were up with her when she was sat down, blanket over her legs. Used to take her to Robert's Park. Used to sit in the shelter an' eat us chips. That all stopped when she had the stroke, mind. Wun't go out at all then. Din't like folk staring at her, what with her face all paralysed down one side an' that.

Yes, spent the last eight year of her life stuck in 'ere; this room where clocks tell their own time. I pick up the picture frame, wipe the front of it down me fleece. S'the photo o'Gran. She's stood on the prom at Morecambe, arm in arm with the woman what bore me. Me Mam before she became "a waste o'space." Twenty when she had me. Two year after that she sodded off and left me with Gran. I touch her face with the tip o'me finger, then breathe on the glass till she disappears. Gone. Quick as she did the day she sodded off and left me. Yeah, childless, me Mam was.

When Gran caught me looking at the photo, she'd say, "I might not have been a looker like you, our Karen, but I looked a right bobby dazzler in that hat, din't I?" And I'd smile at her, wondering what on earth she saw when she looked at me. Something rare maybe, like a flower what bleeds. "But you *was* a looker, Gran," I'd tell her, "an' allus will be, an' all, far as I'm concerned. Now shurrup an' brush yer face!" And we'd laugh. It were our little joke. Us private joke.

I look round the dingy lounge. At the old velvet curtain pulled across the front door. At the draught excluder shaped like a sausage dog. At the gas fire she'd have me clean with an old toothbrush. Rosewater, disinfectant and old hair left to clean itself. Yeah, filthy, the room is. Should run a duster round, but I can't face it. The past - room's thick with it. S'everywhere. I'd never be able to shift it. Turn in her grave though, she would, if she saw how I'd let it go.

Forgot what I've come 'ere fo' now. Oh I know, scissors. There's a pair in Gran's old sewing basket. S'not a sewing basket any more, really. An't been for eight year. Still think of it as that though, call it that. Use it to keep me pens an' stuff in now. S'funny, in't it, how the past's that much stronger than the present. Takes over if yer let it. But I'll not let it, I'll not!

Lounge might still be Gran's, but this room up 'ere's mine. Made it me own. Made it out o'mirrors. Packs and packs o'mirrored tiles from Focus DIY off Baildon Road. Taxi driver what drove me 'ome, winked when I told him they was for me bedroom. Mucky old bugger.

Walls, ceiling, doors – s'all mirrors now. Took me two days to sort it - sticking 'em on, cutting 'em up to fit round the light switches an' that. Worth it though. Lovely in 'ere, it is now. Specially when the sun shines. So bright. I like the light. Like how nice it feels on yer skin. Like to see meself reflected round the room. Up to me eyes in reflections, I am. Left, right, up, straight on. Wherever I look, the truth staring me right in the face. Am perfect now. Chin, nose, eyes, cheekbones, everything. Yeah, am a looker, me now. And not a waste o'space neither. Not after what I did.

I pick up the *Daily Mirror* from the pile o'newspapers I got off the End Shop, and lay it across me lap. BAILED BOYD – THE MOST HATED WOMAN IN BRITAIN? Under the headline, Jude wearing dark glasses. I touch her face with the tip o'me finger. She's giving the Vs out the side winder of a Nissan Micra. Yve's Nissan Micra, looks like.

Under the bed, I can see the box. An old Timpson's shoe box covered in brown paper. I look away, but it catches me eye again in the mirrors opposite. Am on me knees now by the bed, box in front of me, lid off. I crack me knuckles. Inside, a book, a paperback. S'Jude's novel, *The Runner's Daughter*. I pluck it open – the pages are stuck together - then Braille read the biro-ed inscription through the flysheet. I've read the book three times now, cover to cover. Told her I an't though. Don't know why.

I flick through the pages. Words, whole sentences underlined. Notes I've made in the margins. At the back, a piece of paper folded in two. I open it up. RECLAIM THE CUNT, REGAIN THE FEMININE! – A Seminar on Female Beauty led by renowned Feminist-Anarchist, JUDE BOYD. It looks like it's been screwed up, then ironed flat with a fist.

I peer into the box. There's a face. My face with a hole in the middle of it. A compact disc. Across it, written in girlish bubble writing, the words: **How old is my vagina?!** **Plastic Surgery: A Betrayal of the Female.**

Under the CD, a silver ring with red garnet eyes. I slip it on each o'me fingers, even me thumb, but it dun't fit any of 'em. The metal gargoyle sneers at me insolently, so I drop it back in the box. Next to it, a bootlace. Black, chewed-looking. I hold it up by the plastic bit and swallow, remembering the hair - dark, wiry and forked at one end like a snake's tongue. I coil the lace round me fingers and press it to me mouth. It smells musty, feels coarse against me top lip.

Am cross-legged on the bed now, shoe box on one side, Gran's old sewing basket, the other; newspapers everywhere. I pick up the *Guardian*, scan the front page, scissors jawing the air, ready. FEMINIST ANARCHIST DENIES GBH. Biting me tongue, I start cutting round Jude's picture.

Chapter F

It was dark in Karen's bedroom. Just strangled light seeping through the scarf covering the lampshade. A wardrobe, pine with double doors, dominated the left side of the room. Karen was sitting on the floor, scissors in hand, studiously avoiding her reflection in the mirror. Next to her, a pile of glossy magazines, a glue stick, a cap-less bottle of vodka, half-full and a plastic basket full of cosmetics.

"Gynweth's conk first," said Karen, picking up a copy of *Glamour*. "Allus start with the conk, I say."

The scissors hacked through the front cover. Despite the butchery, Gwyneth Paltrow's smile remained resolute. Karen laid the cut-out nose carefully on the carpet, then reached for the vodka.

"C'mere yer bugger," she said, grabbing the air. "Come to momma."

Karen swiped her mouth with her sleeve. "S'better," she said, ears pretending to listen as she talked to herself. "Need a gob, now. Angelina's, gotta be, an't it. Gotta be."

A faint tapping noise on the wall opposite. Frowning, Karen waved it away with the magazine in her hand, and reached for the scissors again.

"Right, s'me gob done. Eyes next."

A banging noise now. Quick, rhythmic, wounding the quiet of the bedroom. "'king 'ell, gerra soddin' room!" she shouted, hands over her ears. "Ha - yeah, all right then, you 'ave, but still…" Slapping sounds, then muted cries.

Karen swallowed. "Eyes. Where are me eyes," she muttered, rifling through the magazine. "Madonna's or that news presenter lass?"

In the middle of the room now, Karen, dancing. Held out in her arms, a full-size poster of Kate Winslet. Karen pulled it towards her and pushed her face through the hole she'd cut out the top. Wedged there, wearing the poster like a paper evening dress, she continued to dance.

"Near, far, wherever y'are, I belieeeeve that the heart does go on," she sang, arms wide, then took a slug of vodka. A captured glimpse of herself in the mirror.

"God sake," she said, ripping the poster off and throwing it on the ground. "S'matter wi' yer, eh? Loser."

Round Karen's neck, a tray, like the ones worn by ice cream sellers in theatres. It was her Gran's. On it, the various facial features she'd cut from the magazines. Carefully, Karen began to stick them onto a sheet of paper pinned to the wardrobe door.

"Job's a good 'un," she said eventually, resting her arms on the tray. She looked at the composite face like it was her own reflected back at her. Her face, but from the future. "Bloody lovely tharr'is."

Karen put the tray on the floor and reached for the vodka. The glass neck had come out in a cold sweat, the Taboo Blue Vodka label curling up at the corners.

"One for the road," she muttered, swigging from the bottle, then bent down and slid the basket of cosmetics towards her. Karen stood up, then lurched forward, knocking the bottle against the wardrobe. Head rush. Swallowing, she pressed the cool glass against her forehead and waited for it to pass.

"Come on," she said eventually and plunged a hand into the slag heap of make-up. A bottle of foundation and a triangle of sponge. Heart racing, Karen looked in the mirror on the other wardrobe door. Her features swirled before her, wouldn't stay still, wouldn't fix in her mind. Karen leaned forward and pressed her forehead to the glass. It felt good to be this close to herself. To be so close that it was like she was no longer there. Sighing, Karen stepped back. On the mirror, a grey balloon like an empty speech bubble. Hands shaking, Karen upended the bottle of foundation, then began to erase the mess of herself with the sponge.

Blank canvas now. Lined up on the carpet, an eyebrow pencil, mascara wand, eyeshadow, highlighter, blusher and lipstick. Karen picked up a lip liner and started to redraw herself. Twenty minutes later, she stepped back and looked from her own face to the composite one she'd been copying. A frown worried her forehead. Karen wasn't how she was supposed to be. She turned away, trying to unsee herself. It was all wrong. She was still all wrong. Karen bared her teeth in the mirror. Small, even, white. They looked useless. Like bricks that don't make anything. She concentrated on not moving her face, keeping it perfectly still. Flaws, everywhere flaws. Karen dabbed at a tiny smudge of red lipstick with the tip of her little finger, then fumbled in her pocket looking for a tissue. Instead, she found a leaflet folded in two. Karen stumbled towards the floor lamp, pulling the scarf off the shade. The vodka bottle she'd knocked over, rolled towards her feet. She opened out the leaflet and tilted it towards the light.

RECLAIM THE CUNT, REGAIN THE FEMININE! – A Seminar on Female Beauty led by renowned Feminist-Anarchist, JUDE BOYD. 12th March, 7pm, Ian Clough Hall, Baildon. For full details on this seminar and other workshops, call 07730 666302.

Back at the mirror, Karen looked from the leaflet in her hand to the fault lines on the face staring back at her.

"Phone, where's me soddin' phone?" she muttered, feeling the front of her jeans. Back pocket. Karen dialled the number on the leaflet, jabbing violently at the keys.

"Jude Boyd?" A deep voice, rich. The kind of voice that had colour – purple, burgundy, cerise.

"Yeah, hiya… hi… so… s'me, I…" Karen's words stumbled out her mouth as if they were running in heels down a cobbled street.

"Well that narrows it down fo' me, dun't it," said Jude. "Can yer be a bit more specific, cos there's a lot o' me's in the world, love."

"Soz… soz, s'Karen… we met… I cleaned up after yer," said Karen, rubbing her eye into a crayoned bruise. "At Shipley Baths."

"Yeah? Right. And?"

"I want… I want to get, yer know, me cunt back," said Karen, squinting at the leaflet in her hand. "Regain the fenimine an' that."

"Well yer sound as pissed as a newt to me, Karen. Tell yer what, you 'ave a nice lie down, yeah, sleep it off. Then if yer still interested when yer come round, give us a ring, eh, cos right now, yer wastin' me fuckin' time!" Jude hung up.

"Bitch," said Karen, snapping the phone shut. The leaflet quivered in her fingers. Karen screwed it into a ball then lobbed it across the room.

Chapter G

Am on me computer. First time in… well since it all blew up, really. Not me computer obviously, that an't blown up. No, all what's happened since we got back from Romania. Not dared go into me emails yet. I know what I'll find. The past. Inbox inundated with it. Me head's throbbing. Throbbing like the cursor. I look away from the screen. Slotted on me finger, the CD from the shoe box. I spin it round till it makes me feel bilious, then I flip it over and look at the handwriting. Her handwriting. **How old is my vagina?!** **Plastic Surgery: A Betrayal of the Female.** Bloated letters, big loops, circles dotting the i's.

I've got me head in me hands. The CD's whirring in the disk drive. Then I hear it, the music. Hendrix riffing the American national anthem. A live version of Patti Smith's *Rock 'n' Roll Nigger*. Jude's theme tune. Through the lats o'me fingers, I watch her appear on screen like Boadicea. She's spotlit in the middle of a big stage. Well, I say big; it's Bingley Little Theatre so hardly soddin'

Wembley. Jude's sat astride a butterfly chair turned back-ards way round. Slowly she stands, arms wide, embracing the audience. Applause. Cheering. Patti singing…

…baby was a black sheep, baby was a whore. You know she got big, well she's gonna get bigger. Baby got a hand, got a finger on the trigger. Baby, baby, baby is a rock 'n' roll nigger…

Jude presses down on the air with her palms till the clapping stops, the singing stops. Silence. Then the sound of her black cowboy boot thumping the chair.

"RECLAIM THE CUNT," she shouts, putting her hands on her hips, nodding defiantly. "REGAIN THE FEMININE. It's time, sisters, yeah? It's long overdue!" More applause.

Jude strides to the edge of the stage, adjusting her head mike.

"You, sister, in the front row," says Jude, pointing at a young woman in a blue top. "How old is your vagina?" The woman looks at her lap. "Come on, don't be shy." Jude moves along the row. "What about you, how old's yours, then, eh? Twelve? Eighteen? Thirty-four?"

"Um…"

"The correct answer, sisters, is your age. Your age on this, the fifteenth day of December 2008 in the year of our Lady. Awomen to that, eh!" Jude strides to the other end of the stage. "Awomen to 34 year-old cunts and 59 year old cunts. Awomen to 18 year old cunts and 82 year old cunts! What do you say?"

"Awomen!" the audience shouts back.

"But these are strange times, evil times, sisters, cos we're livin' in an age where cosmetic gynaecology is on the rise. Can you believe that? Western female genital mutilation is back." Jude nods her head. "Yes, it's official, we've regressed back to the 1850s. The 1850s when clitoridectomy was used to cure women of the so-called moral leprosy of female masturbation. And now it's happening again. Right here, right now, sisters, in two thousand and bloody eight!"

I watch Jude pull at the waistband of her jeans, chest puffed up, cheeks red.

"I mean, is nothing fuckin' sacred any more? Is a woman not allowed to be her age, be herSELF, on the inside now either? Clitoridectomy, cosmetic gynaecology, any kind of plastic surgery," says Jude, gesturing with her arm, "what they're about is the butchering of female flesh. Cutting up the female body to make it conform to an ideal foisted on women by society. And that, in my book, yeah, is an act of violence against women." A burst of applause.

I sneeze a meteor shower on the screen, then hastily wipe it off with me sleeve. This next bit's ace.

"Apparently, women have never had it so good. Well I disagree, cos to my mind, there's no progress in moving from a Victorian age that shames female sexuality, to one that shames women who don't look like fuckin' Barbie! Female flesh – or *fat* as it's usually described nowadays – has replaced female desire as public enemy number one in our society. Women's bodies, it seems, must be controlled and contained at all costs."

Jude plays with the piercing in her left eyebrow.

"Last year, the British cosmetic surgery industry was worth over £400 million. £400 *million*, can you believe that? That's nearly 200,000 operations a year. That's nearly 200,000 women - cos let's not forget, most cosmetic surgery consumers are female – nearly 200,000 women needlessly putting themselves under the knife every year. What's all that about, then, eh? Well I'll tell you what it's NOT about, sisters." Jude stands centre-stage now. "It's not about personal empowerment, that's for sure. It's not about women enjoying freedom of choice. CHOICE?! Don't make me fuckin' laugh!"

Jude climbs on top of the chair, opens her arms, then jumps off.

"That, my friends, was me enjoying freedom of choice. *I* chose to climb on the chair and jump off, without any influence from any bugger else. Free will in action, sisters. Us women though, we're being forced to make decisions about our bodies influenced by a society that says some choices are better than others. A society that says facial lines, pot bellies, sagging breasts an' slackened cunts, are barriers to happiness. A society that effectively says women's bodies aren't allowed to show their life experiences. So, women who choose to have plastic surgery, then are not making a genuinely free choice." Jude jabs her finger at the audience. "And that's not all. Some women - some of them so-called feminists - are so in love with this idea of women now having a "choice" over how they look, they're willing to defend ANY action a woman takes to alter her body."

"Cosmetic surgery isn't about giving women choice. That's bollocks! It's time for a few home truths, sisters. Let me tell you how it *really* is - surgical beautification is extreme self-indulgence and man-pleasing. Nothing more, nothing less."

I press the pause button and rub me eyes. Mouth feels like the inside of an old gardening glove. I open the desk drawer, looking for a stray polo mint or a stick o'gum. Nothing. I roll me shoulders then crack me knuckles. Play.

"The cosmetic surgery industry, though would have us believe otherwise. And you know how they've done it? They've done exactly what the media and beauty industry have been doing for years. They've taken the feminist call for the empowerment of women, repackaged it and sold it back to us." Jude shakes her head. "The cosmetic surgery industry has effectively STOLEN the feminist call to arms, and used it to create consumer feminism. How dare they! How fuckin' dare they use the feminist call for freedom of choice to sell cosmetic surgery. How dare they steal our core message to sell facelifts and tit jobs as self determinism. How did that happen, eh? Why the FUCK have we let that happen?!"

Muttering, the audience shifting in their seats.

"The media – advertising, articles in magazines, reality TV make-over shows – they'd all have us believe cosmetic surgery is as benign and mundane as whitening your teeth or colouring your hair. Not true. They'd have us believe cosmetic procedures are an effortless, egalitarian way for women of all backgrounds to enhance their looks, and stay young. Not so. They'd have us hail plastic surgeons - 98% of whom are men - as the new Gods, as saviours of the feminine. Total bollocks!"

Jude swipes at the sweat glistening on her forehead.

"It's time to tell it like it is, sisters. Do you want the truth?!"

"Yes!"

"I can't hear you. Do you want the truth?"

"YES!"

Jude pinches the corners of her mouth and prowls menacingly from one side of the stage to the other.

"Cosmetic surgery is a symptom of something much bigger than the body and individual choice. It's a symptom of faulty self-identity and an obsession with celebrity. Plastic surgery is a symptom of a moral authority that's been transferred from the medical profession to the commercial media. And that, to my mind, is an outrage and downright dangerous. In this age of materialistic consumerism, a face-lift will always make sense as a lifestyle choice. But, like I said, us women have no real choice in the matter. The media and the beauty and cosmetic surgery industries, they've all hoodwinked us into thinking we have autonomy over our bodies." Jude adjusts the angle of her mike. "You know what I'd like, sisters? I'd like the choice NOT to consider having cosmetic surgery. In fact I demand that fuckin' right!"

Jude plucks at the neck of her t-shirt. I slide forward in me chair and swallow. This is me favourite bit.

"So, how we gunna stop this gravy train, then eh? Cos the cosmetic surgery market just keeps on growing, sisters. 48% a year since the year 2000. Us women can't get enough of it, can we, eh? But like I said, we've been duped. Duped into spending us hard-earned cash on surgery we don't need. Surgery that does more harm than good, even kills in some cases. But it's time we said NO! No more! What's it time we said?"

"NO MORE!"

"That's right. And only WE can stop this gravy train, sisters. Us women. Cos rest assured, the media with its TV ads and its endless make-over reality shows, they ain't gonna kill off this golden goose, that's for sure. And as for the Government, their only concern is to tighten up the regulations so consumers feel more confident about spending their money on it."

"No, it's down to us. Down to every last one of us women to embrace who we are, ALL we are. Every wrinkle, every extra pound, every stretch mark, every single imper-fuckin-fection. And the time is now, sisters, cos a recession can only work in our favour. People an't got the money they had, to waste on things they don't need. And uncertainty in the financial markets has made easy credit a thing of the past. No, the time is now, sisters. Reclaim the cunt!"

"RECLAIM THE CUNT!"

"Regain the feminine!"

"REGAIN THE FEMININE!"

I press pause. A freeze-frame of Jude, arms wide, reaching out. I can feel her. Feel her hands holding me face, me new face, and I smile. Yeah, I love yer too, Mam.

Chapter H

Karen was standing in the foyer, a pause of dead space between the main hall and the car park. Barking and shouting, that was all she could hear. A Jack Russell complaining about being tied up outside, and a woman's voice belting out through a PA system. Karen had her hands tucked in the sleeves of her anorak, one trainer resting on the other. Next to her, two empty chairs, a table limping under the weight of a pile of books, and Jude Boyd – a life-size cardboard cut-out. The folded arms and fierce, violet eyes gave her a solidity at odds with the one-dimensional outline wavering in the breeze from the front door.

The seminar had already started when Karen arrived at Ian Clough Hall. She looked at her Gran's watch. Nearly over. They'd be out soon. Karen moved away from the doors to the main hall, and stood in front of Jude, tentatively reaching out a hand to touch her arm. Applause, chairs scraping, footsteps, eager chatter. Karen pulled up her hood and scuttled across the foyer, feigning interest in a poster for the Baildon Players' upcoming performance of *Madame Butterfly*. People, mainly women, milled around or filed past.

"If you'd care to buy Jude's novel from me at this end of the table," Yve called, gesturing at the pile of paperbacks in front of her. "You can then make your way to the other end, where Jude will gladly sign it for you."

Karen was three away from Jude, last in the queue. In her hands, a copy of *The Runner's Daughter*.

The pages thrummed under her thumb, releasing a woody, fibrous scent. Peering over the top of the book, Karen's eyes scanned Jude like a bar coder – dreadlocks scraped back off her face; dark grey eye make-up; nose ring glinting in the overhead light; purple mouth edged with black lip liner; huge diamante cross nestled in the ravine of her cleavage.

"Any more for any more?" Jude twirled the black biro between her fingers like a majorette's baton. The pen clicked rhythmically against her rings. Then, seeing Karen dithering with a book in her hands, said, "oi, lady, look sharp." Karen fiddled with the toggle of her hood. Down or pull it up again? Down. Leave it down. She stepped towards the desk.

"Arright?" said Jude, plucking the book from Karen's reluctant hands. "I'll just sign me name, shall I, or d'yer want me to write sommat else?"

"I'd… I'd like… can yer write to Karen from Jude… with love." Her eyes were fixed on the folds in the orange curtain behind Jude's head. "Please. Ta."

Jude sniffed, then pressed the front cover back firmly with her fist. "To… Karen," she wrote slowly. Big, girlish bubble writing.

"I wish I'd been called something a bit more exotic," said Karen, chewing her lip. "Woulda like to've been named after a hurricane, sommink like that. But Karen it is, so… Still, coulda been worse, cun't it. Coulda been called Ethel or… or Knobchucker or sommat…"

Jude looked up. "Are you that lass what rung me, pissed as a newt?" She grinned. Her teeth were surprisingly small and pointed. "It were, weren't it. You're that cleaning lass from the other night - I recognise yer face."

Karen blushed at the carpet tiles, then nodded sheepishly.

"Oi, Yve. It's that cleaning lass from Shipley Baths, remember?"

Yve came over and stood next to Jude, hand on the back of her chair. "Of course, yes. Hello again." Yve's face smiled, then decided not to. "Oh, is… I think you've got something…a bit of food on your…" Yve pointed at her own chin, eyes squinting. Karen, suddenly acutely aware of the blood in her cheeks, pressed a hand to her mouth. "Oh, I'm sorry," said Yve, fiddling with her necklace. "Forgive me. I'm as blind as a bat without my specs, aren't I, Jude."

"Not much better with," Jude replied. Her eyes scrutinised Karen's face like the hands of a blind person.

"I… I saw you at The Candy Club other night an' all," said Karen, hurriedly. She pulled the neck of her anorak up round her mouth, eyes flicking between Jude and the ladies' room to her right. "Bloody brilliant what you did in there, what yer said to them men."

"What the fuck were *you* doing at The Candy Club?" Jude said, snapping the top back on her pen.

"I were just… I just went in to… I mean, I'd heard about places like that, about pole dancing an' that," said Karen, looking at the book Jude had signed for her. "An't ever been in one though. Wanted to see fo' meself, see if it were as bad as I thought. It were worse. Dead shocked, I was."

"Yeah, shit holes, them clubs. Me and Yve had it planned for months, that little demo at The Candy Club." Jude slid Karen's book across the desk then stood up. "We're gonna do some other stuff, more demos an' that. If yer up for gerrin involved, we'll be at the Old Glen House tomorra from seven."

Karen picked up her book and nodded. "That's the pub near the Glen Railway, in't it?"

"The very same," said Jude, pulling out a sheaf of dreads from inside her leather trench coat. "See yer there tomorra, then."

Yve frowned at Jude's back as they headed out to the car park. "Why on earth did you invite *her* along?" Yve said, looking up at the rain stammering on the overhead canopy. "We hardly know the girl."

"I dunno, Yve," said Jude, shrugging. "There's just… something about 'er."

Karen read the inscription on the flysheet then turned the page, describing Jude's writing with her fingertip. She zipped up her anorak, the book tucked away inside it. Karen could feel her heart thumping against the weight of pages. "See you there, then," she whispered, trying on the words she'd wanted to say a minute ago, but couldn't find. Something on the carpet caught her eye. Long, black. A bootlace. Karen bent down and picked it up. Jude's bootlace. There was a long strand of dark, wiry hair wound around it. Gripping the lace firmly in her fist, Karen headed for the door.

*

What was left of the ice had melted in the soap dish. Straining through the bathroom door, PJ Harvey. Music to hurt yourself by. On the floor next to Karen, an empty bottle of ASDA Smart Price vodka, a needle and a bloodied towel. Karen peered down at the shaving mirror wedged between her knees. In her hand, a paring knife. She'd just cut round the mole on her chin and was lifting it off with the point of the blade. Pretty violence. Teeth clenched, jaw set. Her left eye was streaming.

"I think you've got something a bit of food on your… I think you've got something a bit of food on your…," she chanted, then flinched. "Ah, soddin' hell!" She bit her lip. "Pain is… fuck! Pain is just a point of view painisjustapointofview."

Pain is something Karen knows well. So well, she's always one step ahead of it. Looking at a knife, she can feel the pain before it cuts, like the blade is the pain.

On the tip of the knife, her mole. With the towel, Karen dabbed at the seeping red hole in the middle of her chin. "Did it, I did it," she whispered, resting back against the towel rail. A smile haunted her face then passed through to the back of her head. Hanging from the rail, her anorak. It dripped abstractly on the cork tiles. Her eyelids slowly flickered closed. Such peace in knives.

Suddenly alert, Karen fumbled in her anorak pocket for the bootlace and her signed copy of *The Runner's Daughter*. Holding the front cover back with her leg, Karen edged the mole from the blade onto the first page. Then, after unwinding the dark wire of hair from it, she laid the bootlace along the seam of the book.

"There," she said, nodding, and pushed down on the front cover with the flat of her hand.

Strings of red oozed from the hole down her chin. Reaching for the needle, she threaded the hair through its eye and knotted the end. "Nice an' easy," she whispered, then with quivering hands, began to sew up the wound.

Chapter 1

I've turned me phone back on. Nothing, thank God. She's not called or texted or owt. Not since this morning. Reckon she's got the message. I like that. Like how silence says more than any words could. Yeah, nothing, thank God. No calls or texts or owt. Still here though. The past. S'all over me soddin' floor. Newspapers, big holes cut out of 'em, all over me soddin' floor. Newspapers telling tales. Coercion. Exploitation. Mutilation. Tales with big holes in 'em. Am looking at one now. Front page o'the *Yorkshire Post*. There's a picture o'me. One from the video. On the internet. A picture from the video on the internet. There's this bit about Jude:

'... *little known outside her native Yorkshire, Jude Boyd has had a varied career - performance poet, novelist, founder of a now defunct small women's press, tattoo artist, and an activist on women's issues.*'

... *little known outside her native Yorkshire* – she'll not like that. The reporter claims to have an exclusive. The inside story straight from the horse's gob. Well, it's an horse what does its muck out the wrong 'ole then, s'all I can say. Kidnapped, my arse. Drugged?! I soddin' wish. I swirl a hand in the dry pool of newsprint next to me, and shake me head. They an't got a clue, them journalists. Not about me anyway. They don't know owt, not really, cos I've kept schtum. They only know what Jude's told 'em. And she dun't know owt either. Not what am like, where I live, nobody does. Made sure o'that. Like to keep meself to meself. Allus have. Prefer me own company to other folk's. Things allus get messy round other folk. I get messy.

According to the *Telegraph & Argus* what's just come through the door, I'm in a safe-house somewhere in Leeds. The *Yorkshire Evening Post* disagrees; reckons I'm in a private hospital out Ilkley way, convalescing after me ordeal. I hold the page up and look through the hole. I can see right through it. Right through it to the truth, cos what *really* happened's right there in the mirror. Perfect I am now, not all broken up in bits, like what the press says. I'll not read any more though now, I've decided.

Outside, it's dropping dark. Got the bedroom lamps on. All of 'em. Happy light. There's sommat about it, lamplight. The starkness of it. I like it. Like how nice it feels on yer skin. Up to me eyes in reflections, I am. Wherever I look, the truth staring me right in the face. Perfect I am now. Chin, nose, eyes, cheekbones, everything. Yeah, am a looker, me now. And not a waste o'space neither. Not after what I did. "Soddin' hell!"

Phone. S'Jude screaming her name at me from the screen. JUDE. Allus shouting she is, mouthing off. I don't know what to do… can't decide. Dithering. "H-hello?"

"Hi… Karen? Well, about fuckin' time an' all! Where the bloody 'ell have yer been, eh? Eh?! Why haven't you answered me calls or me texts or… ?" I swallow, look at the phone in me hand. "Have you not read the papers? Have you not seen what they're saying about me?"

I want the silence back. I like that. Like how silence says more than any words could.

"HELLO?! Is yer mobile broke, is that it, eh? Fuckin' answer me, Karen!"

Allus shouting Jude is, mouthing off. Shouldn't have answered. I don't know what to do… can't decide. Dithering.

"Karen, am on me own wi' all this, yeah. Am havin' to *deal* with this all on me own. Yve's fucked off, you know. It were probably 'er what told all them lies to the papers." She swallows. "I could go to prison, Karen, d'you understand?"

I wipe me mouth, look at the phone, put it to me ear again.

"You can't do this to me, Karen. I won't fuckin' let yer, you hear me?" A deep breath, ragged. "Can I come an' see yer? Where are yer, Karen? Christ, I don't even know where yer bloody live. Look, we need to talk. Let's meet, yeah, try an' sort this out, decide what to do. Karen?"

"All right." I look round the room. Left, right, up, straight on. Who said "all right"? Which one o'me said "all right"?

"Yeah? G-good, that's good, Karen. Where? Just… just tell me where an' I'll meet yer, okay?"

"Cow an' Calf."

"Cow an' Calf Rocks? What the fuck you want to meet up there fo'?"

"S'quiet."

"Okay, well, okay, when then?"

"Tomorra. Dawn."

"Dawn?! No, I can't… s'too early, Karen. Dun't give me enough time… I won't have time to… Later though, yeah? How about ten? Ten o'clock, Cow an' Calf Rocks."

"All right."

Chapter J

The air like dry ice in her mouth. Karen was climbing the path next to Shipley Glen's funicular tramway. The cable that pulled day trippers up the sharp incline on weekends, lay rusty and silent in the middle of the track. Dotted along its quarter-mile length, the odd cut-out snowman left over from the Santa Special three months before. Karen straightened the tongue of her trainer then pushed on, past the old dodgem ride with its pile-up of cars, and the shut-up souvenir shop. On open days, there was a sweet machine out front with a stuffed parrot inside that wolf-whistled at passers-by.

Nestled in the wooded valley below Baildon Moor, a long, low building made of weathered Yorkshire stone. The Old Glen House pub. Along its length, spotlights picked out the gold letters of its name. Karen looked at the time - 19.05 - and at the pub's front entrance. Then she carried on walking, past the public toilets boarded up with plywood, and on to where the light from the street lamp, like a slick of orangeade, ran out. Karen sat down on a boulder, her back to the wooded ravine. In the grass by her trainer, a discarded condom, yellow and withered. She nudged it with her toe, then stole another look at the time. They'd be in there by now, chatting, drinking. Karen's leg juddered. She rested her arms on her thighs, hands squeezed between her knees. Wrapped four times round one wrist, the black bootlace. Karen fiddled with the knot, pulling on the plastic ends, then stood up and headed back to the pub.

"The thing is, yeah, most so-called feminists today are as ball-less as men. There's no fight in 'em any more," said Jude, wrestling her dreads into an elastic band. "Reactive and tokenistic, that's what the feminist movement's become. At best. S'enough to make yer fuckin' weep!"

Karen gulped her vodka and coke, eyes fixed on the tattooed flames licking Jude's neck. Beneath them, letters, numbers – BCFC 11.05.85 EXIT K.

"Reactive and tokenistic? That's a bit harsh, Jude," said Yve, glass of red wine poised in her hand.

"A bit harsh? I don't fuckin' think so. All right, answer me this then, Yve… both of yer." Jude waved a dog-eared beer mat at them. Karen swallowed like she was dropping anchor. On her face, the look of someone not ready to be listened to. "Name one thing the feminist movement has done in the last thirty-odd year what's made a difference. I mean on the scale of, like Women's Suffrage or Women's Lib. When in the last thirty-odd year have you seen feminists anywhere in the world, come out *en masse* to stand up for women's rights? Hmm? Answer me that."

"Well, I can't think of…"

"Exactly, Yve!" said Jude, slapping the table. Her pint of Guinness jumped, beheading itself. "Which is fuckin' pitiful when you think about the level of subjugation women all over the world are *still* having to put up with."

"S'right that," said Karen, picking at the plaster on her chin. "Them women in burkas what you see in Bradford city centre, walking ten steps behind their husbands an' that. Yer don't hear no feminists standing up for them, now do yer. Saying how criminal it is in this day an' age."

"No, yer bloody don't. That's because feminism is, and arguably allus has been, white and middle class. Which means it's only ever been fussed about white an' middle class issues," said Jude, taking a swig of her pint. "What yer done to yer chin, then?"

"I cut it… s'just a cut," said Karen, hastily taking a sip of her vodka and coke.

"I think the problem is this," said Yve, smoothing the front of her velvet skirt, "feminism just doesn't seem relevant anymore. Not to women under thirty-five anyway. Young women today enjoy more freedom than any other generation of women before them. As far as they're concerned, they can do whatever they want… and generally do, if what you see on the telly is anything to go by. So, looking at it from their point of view, what's left to fight for?"

"What's left to fight for?! Well, the right to look and be who they really are, for starters. The right to age, to get old. The right to be fuckin' *real!*" said Jude, shredding the beer mat.

"Yes, yes, I'm with you. I agree with you, Jude, but then I'm in my fifties. I was part of the Women's Lib movement when I was at art school. What I'm talking about, though is young women *today*. As far as they're concerned, there's nothing to make a stand about." Yve fluffed up her hair and looked at Jude over the top of her glasses.

"Yve, the very things you were making a stand about in the early seventies – sexist images of women in the popular media, sexual freedom, abortion, pornography," said Jude, counting them off on her fingers, "still hold true today, cos nothing's changed. In fact, it's got worst in my view, thanks to the internet. What underpinned Women's Lib in the sixties and seventies, was women's bodies. That was the basis of the struggle for liberation. But look in any newsagent's today – and not the top shelf neither, cos it's right in front o'yer face – look at all the porn on the internet, look at the women young girls aspire to be, Jordan and that skinny fuckin' Beckham lass. The same things what made you and millions of other women take to the streets thirty-odd year ago, Yve, are the very reason women under thirty-five should be doing the same today. They should be up in fuckin' arms," said Jude, shaking her head.

Yve nodded. "Actually, you're right."

"Too bloody right, I'm right," said Jude. "Us women are being constantly undermined, and in very subtle, clever ways an' all. Walk down any high street, turn on your telly, go online and there they are - subliminal messages about how we're supposed to look and behave. They're every fuckin' where." Jude played with her rings. "And the fight to undermine us has got really ugly, in my view, cos they're using all the things we've fought for over the years – freedom to express our sexuality, freedom to choose – to oppress us."

"Who d'yer mean by *they*, then?" said Karen, frowning.

"Them what's in positions of power in the media and in the beauty, fashion an' plastic surgery industries - fuckin' MEN of course, thanks to the glass bloody ceiling." Jude drained her pint, waved her glass at the bar man and pointed at the other empties on the table. "They're laughin' at us, blokes are, and rubbing their bloody hands together an' all. You want freedom to express your sexuality, ladies? Well, that's fine by us blokes. Express it all over us laps when yer dance fo' us in't clubs we're opening up on every high street. Express it all over us lads' mags, cos it's all just a bit o'harmless fun, in't it, spreading yer legs an' stroking yer tits for the whole world to see."

The bar man put the drinks down, collected the empties in his fleshy claw then left, Jude's ten pound note hanging from his mouth like a parched tongue.

"Want to express your freedom to choose, ladies?" Jude continued, carving her initial in the top of her Guinness, "fine by us blokes. Express it by doing whatever it takes to stay young an' beautiful, so we'll not fuck off wi' someone half yer age, an' bigger tits, the first chance we get."

Karen took a hasty sip of her vodka and coke then added, "not that yer'll be able to express it though, ladies. Not on yer face any road, cos it'll be so full o'Botox yer'll not be able to move it."

Jude smirked into her beer. "Too fuckin right, our Karen! 'ere, yer should 'ave a watch o'this." Jude pulled a CD out of her bag. "Yer'll love it," she said, handing it to Karen. "It's me doing me *How old is my vagina!?* seminar. Fuckin' classic, it is, in't it Yve?"

Yve nodded abstractly, then returning to the earlier theme, added, "well I guess the million dollar question is, how do you get women, young women I mean, to wake up to what's happening and fired up enough to do something about it?"

"You fight fire with fire, Yve, that's what yer do. You use the same armoury the enemy's using against women i.e. the media. The internet's done a lot to undermine us, but it can empower us an' all. We just need to wise up an' make it work fo' us. YouTube, blogs, Twitter, Facebook, Myspace – they can be our weapons too. The internet allows anyone, anywhere to get their message across to millions o'people at the push of a button. An' that means me… us three. Thanks to the internet, Jude Boyd of Eldwick in West fuckin'Yorkshire has the means to make the world take a long, hard look in the mirror. Us three, living up 'ere at the arse end of nowhere, have the power to make the whole world stand up an' take notice."

"How though, Jude? What can we do to get people's attention - millions of people's attention?" said Yve, polishing her specs on the hem of her skirt.

"Fuck, I don't know, Yve. Something bold though. Something controversial, radical."

"Sommat yer wouldn't expect," said Karen, fiddling with her plaster again. "There were this clip on YouTube what was doing the rounds not s'long back. Someone had this video o'the Queen on a visit to some canning factory in Grimsby. As she's walking back to the car, like, there's this noise what sounds like a fart. The Queen farting! Got millions o'hits, that did."

Yve rolled her eyes and smoothed her skirt. Jude slapped her thigh. "Ha! Yeah, something unexpected, that's *exactly* what we need. Something to make folk go out their way to 'ave a look, and then tell other folk about it an' all."

"Yeah, that's what-yer-call-it, in't it - virus marketing," Karen said, cheeks flushed with blood and vodka.

"Exactly! Come on, let's throw some ideas around. What can we do that's controversial an' unexpected. Yve?"

"Err… oh gosh, I'm not very good off the top of my head… umm, how about repeating what we did at The Candy Club. There's that new pole dancing place opening soon on Bingley town street. We could film the demo, then publish it on the interweb."

Jude, leaning on the table, nodded slowly. "Maybe… maybe… not bad."

"Nah, it needs to be way more bold than that, I reckon," said Karen, pressing a beer mat to her cheek. "I mean, s'interestin' like, but it's not radical enough, is it?"

"Yeah, you're right, our Karen. Subject-wise, though, Yve, you're on the right track. Whatever we do it needs to be about women's bodies. That should be our battleground. Like it were in the sixties for us sisters in the Women's Lib. Yeah, the sexploitation an' mutilation of women's bodies in the name of beauty and perpetual youth. That's what we should focus on. Come on, more ideas. Owt, just say the first bloody thing what comes into yer 'eads." Jude pulled a notebook out of her bag.

"Oh, I don't know… um… storm the making of a porn film, you know, disrupt it?" said Yve, sitting on her hands. "Or… or we could build a mountain of lads' mags outside the Houses of Parliament and set fire to them."

Jude's pen shaped the ideas onto the page. "Good… good… keep going keep going. What else?"

"How 'bout filming someone having, like extreme plastic surgery. Sommat like that," said Karen, pressing down on the tremor in her knee.

Jude looked up sharply from her notepad. "Fuckin' ell!" She whacked the table with her hand. "That's it, our Karen. That's fuckin' it! Cosmetic surgery what makes you ugly," she said, drawing speech marks in the air round the last word. "A video of someone havin' plastic surgery what makes 'em look the complete opposite to the way us women are told we should look."

"Well, that's all very interesting, Jude, clever, but come on, be realistic. No one in their right mind would agree to do that," said Yve, wine glass hovering. "And no surgeon would agree to it either."

"Yeah… yeah, I hear yer. But think about. It'd be like the ultimate act of martyrdom. The chance to be a modern day Joan of fuckin' Arc!" Jude held her pen up like a sword. "But as for no doctor agreeing to do it, get real, Yve. There's plastic surgeons all over Eastern Europe champing at the bit to attract Western money with their cut-price facelifts and tit jobs. Just look at the classifieds in any women's glossy, pages of 'em. They can't get women over there fast enough."

"Well, okay, maybe you're right, but the fact remains, there isn't a woman alive who'd be prepared to make that kind of sacrifice."

Karen swallowed and wiped her mouth. "I'd… me… I'll… I'll do it."

Chapter K

Am stood on the edge o'Cow an' Calf Rocks, drunk from running up the hill. She better not be late or I'll catch me death. Catching yer death. Funny turn o'phrase that, in't it. Like death's this solid thing yer can hold in yer hands. I huddle inside me anorak, feeling the ghost of a conversation I an't had yet, walk through me. The sky's trying to be the ground, dropping swathes of grey everywhere. In the distance, I can hear a plane flying in towards Leeds-Bradford Airport. S'like everything up wants to be down. 09:51. There's no one about. Am on me own. Just me and the breeze. A sharp breeze like whispered lies. S'how I like it though. No one about. Prefer me own company to other folk's. Things allus get messy round other folk. I get messy.

"Well, yer picked a right fuckin' spot up 'ere, Karen Backhouse."

I turn round and there's Jude, cheeks flushed, sheen on her top lip and forehead. She opens her trench coat, flapping it. Wings. Like the leathery wings of a big, ancient bird.

"So, 'ow… 'ow've yer bin, then?" she asks the space over me right shoulder.

S'new this. I an't never seen her nervous before. S'unsettling. She's four feet away. Between us, four feet of air what feels like it's been rubbed down with sandpaper.

"Fine, ta. Good," I say, nodding. Me eyes are glued to hers, but Jude won't look at me. She's hardly blinking. "You?"

Jude smirks, kicks a stone away with her cowboy boot. "Me? Oh, am grand me, Karen. On top of the fuckin' world, me!" she says, spreading her arms. A pause. "It wan't supposed to be like this, yer know," she says eventually, looking at her feet. "I just wanted to get people's attention. Not like this, though. It… it were supposed to be about the cause, women's rights. I was… we were fighting for a woman's right to have control over her body, weren't we. But the bastard media's just made it about me." She laughs and shakes her head, dreads shifting wearily round her shoulders. "Of course they've made it about me. Making me out to be a mutilating butcher what preys on vulnerable girls, sells more fuckin' papers, dun't it."

I press me hands to me face. "Maybe, yeah, I guess."

"All I've ever wanted, Karen, was to do something worthwhile. For the world to know who I am. Cos me Mam, yeah she dun't give a toss who I am… or me Dad, whoever the bloody 'ell he was. Buggered off, the pair of 'em, an' I got put into care."

I nod. I know all this. *The Runner's Daughter.* "You know what I think though, Jude? I reckon… I mean, well, maybe the cause yer fighting for - women's rights, animal rights, whatever - in't the one yer think yer fighting for at all." Jude frowns. "At the end o'the day, like, I reckon all causes are really just about yerself. Mainly, anyway, don't yer think, Jude? The real fight is *with* yerself and… and *for* yerself, in't it? At the end o'the day."

Christ, she's soddin' crying now. I've made her cry. Tears like black blood. In me head I'm touching her face. But then I see they're tears of anger. Angry tears what make her cheeks burn red.

"Oh that's great that is. Thanks, Karen. Thanks a lot! Yer've just reduced me whole life, thirty-odd year worth o'work, to a fuckin' ego trip." She swipes at the tears with the heel of each hand. "Where do you get off saying that to me, eh? I mean 'ho the fuck are you, any road?" Jude jabs a finger at me. "An' where *were* yer, when I needed yer to open yer gob an' say sommat to the press? Sommat useful like the truth."

I look at her hands, feel them pushing me off Cow an' Calf Rocks.

"Yer just fuckin' left me to deal with it all, din't yer. Yve an' all. Why, eh? I thought we was a team. I thought we was in this together?"

There's words writing themselves in me head. Writing on the wall inside me head. I LEFT YER COS YER SODDIN' LEFT ME. SODDED OFF AN' LEFT ME WITH GRAN, DIN'T YER, YER SODDIN WASTE O'SPACE!

Eventually me mouth opens and some other words come out, better words. "So, w-when did Yve leave yer, then? Thought I saw her in't paper, pickin' yer'up from't police station."

"Yeah, she picked me up, but that were that, her parting shot. Dun't want anything to do wi' me now, wi' any o'this… not now she's said her three penneth to the press. God, I can't believe she said I took advantage o'yer, of yer condition." Jude fiddles with her rings, twisting 'em round her fingers. "I din't know you was body dysmorphic, Karen, so how could I take advantage."

"Body dys…?" I an't got a clue what she's talking about. "I an't got a clue what yer talking about, Jude. I an't got a condition. It were my choice to go to Bucharest. I wanted to 'ave it done," I say, pointing at her. "Joan of Arc, remember. The ultimate sacrifice."

Jude closes her eyes and nods. "A-fuckin'-men to that," she says, eventually, tears welling in her eyes. "Finally. Thank you, Karen. I mean it, thank you." She pulls something out of her pocket. S'a tape machine. A little tape recorder.

"This way, Karen!"

Clicking, flashes, shouting.

"Karen!"

"Over 'ere, love!"

"Look this way!"

Don't know where to look. I don't… I just… I don't know what to do. I turn this way, that, looking for Jude. Gone. I look at the moor, the rocks, at the edge o'the rocks. I look at me hands, turning 'em this way, that. Looking for that solid thing yer can hold in yer hands. Nothing. Am on me own. On me own with the clicking, the flashes, the shouting, the betrayal. S'just me. Me and twenty-odd photographers stealing me face; me new face. I pull up me hood, wanting to fold up the moor like a tablecloth. Wanting to fold it all away like the last picnic. I look at the moor, the rocks, the edge of the rocks, me hands. Looking for that solid thing yer can hold in yer hands. Then I run.

Chapter L

Standing in front of Karen, a man, drawing on her face with a black marker pen. Karen didn't know where to look. It felt strange, like having a surreal kind of portrait done – her face, the canvas; the artist, a doctor. He was breathing through his nose. Short, sharp breaths. Karen could see the dark hairs in his nostrils being sucked, blown, sucked, blown.

Outside in the corridor, raised voices. Nurses probably, Karen thought. A professional disagreement. She tuned them out, focusing instead on the ache in her arm. Going by the clock on the wall, she'd been holding up the picture for nearly fifteen minutes. Over the doctor's shoulder, a mirrored cabinet. Karen could see her own face and, right next to it, the one she was holding up. The composite face she'd made from the magazines.

"Is good," said the doctor, knees bent, eyes flicking between Karen's face and the cut-up. "Soon, is all done. Then you are looking, yes?"

"Sound as a pound," said Karen. Then, seeing the frown on the doctor's face added, "good… cheers… ta… I mean thanks."

The marker pen felt strangely cold as it drew under her eyes, round her mouth, along her cheeks. It smelled of metallic fruit and made her eyes water. Karen blinked and gripped the edge of the bed. Despite wearing only a hospital gown – a child's, pink with a teddy bear motif – she was sweating. The air in the room, uncomfortable, cloying. "Relax. Is good." The doctor grinned, teeth like crooked gravestones.

Down the corridor, Jude was leaning against the wall, paint and plaster crumbling beneath her palms. Standing opposite, Yve, shaking her head.

"This… it's wrong, Jude. It doesn't… I don't know, it just doesn't feel right," said Yve, shifting her knitted bag onto the other shoulder. Jude stared at her, suddenly irritated by the floaty skirts, the rubber shoes and the way she fiddled with the crystal round her neck.

"Well, we're 'ere now, Yve, so…" said Jude, folding her arms.

"But that doesn't mean it's too late… we can stop this right now," said Yve, looking down the corridor. "All we have to do is walk back in that room and say we've changed our minds."

"*We've* changed us minds?! No, *you* fuckin' have, Yve. Let's be clear about that." Jude shook her head. "You allus were flaky."

Yve bit her thumbnail and looked at the pocked flooring. "I just think… I mean, we don't know anything about her, Jude. Not really. We've met her, what, four, five times? We don't even know where she lives. She had us meet her at the airport instead of coming with us in the taxi. Doesn't that strike you as odd? She's… she's strange, Jude, I…"

"Oh Yve, now you're being paranoid. So she wanted to make her own way there, enjoy her last bit of freedom before being cooped up with us for two week. What's strange about that?"

"All right but… it still feels wrong, Jude. I just don't think she's right for this. I think she has… issues… body issues," said Yve, gripping her elbows.

"Well what woman *dun't* have body issues. Jesus Christ, that's why we're doing this, remember. To make a stand for authenticity. For a woman's right to be herself."

"Yes, but… I think Karen's issues are more complicated than that. She's… I think she has a distorted body image. I think she's… I think she might have body dysmorphia. I mean, I'm no doctor or anything, but from what I've seen…"

"Yeah, that's right, Yve, you're no doctor. Let's not lose sight of that. Listen, from what **I've** seen of Karen, I'm happy she's doing this for the right reasons. She knows exactly what she's doing an' she's doing it off her own bat. She an't been forced to do anything." Jude folded her arms. "She wants to do it, Yve, an' frankly, we're bloody lucky to 'ave her. That lass in there's got more fuckin' bottle than anyone I've ever come across," said Jude, gesturing over her shoulder with her thumb. "So sort yer face out, an' then let's get back in there an' give her the support she deserves, yeah?"

Yve swallowed then nodded, handing Jude the video camera while she looked in her bag for a tissue.

Karen was lying on the bed, staring up at herself in the glass moon of a hand mirror. Her mouth wanted to smile, but she wouldn't let it. Didn't want to ruin the black lines, distort them. "This is how a life begins," she whispered, stroking her cheek. "The next time I touch this face, me hand'll feel like a bird, me skin like air."

"All right, our Karen?" Jude stopped abruptly by the door as Karen lowered the mirror. "Christ… so…so he's done then, the doctor?"

"Aye, they're coming to pick us up in a bit. Five minutes, he said. Gonna wheel me down on the bed."

From the doorway, Yve pointed back out into the corridor, face ashen, eyes blinking rapidly. "I'll… I'll wait outside… let you know when they're on their way."

The door clicked shut.

"Right, well, this is it, kiddo," said Jude, sitting on the end of the bed.

"Yeah, no going back now. I've started so I'll finish an' all that," said Karen, smirking.

Jude took hold of Karen's hand. It looked so frail and bony, like a bat's wing. She wondered how it had the strength to pick anything up.

"I want you to know, our Karen, I think you're one of the bravest, strongest women I've ever met."

"Oh, give over!" Karen fiddled with the neck of her hospital gown.

"No, I mean it, Karen. What you're doing 'ere, today, is one of the most selfless things anyone's ever done. A coupla weeks from now when you've had time to convalesce, people are gonna hear about this great thing yer've done. I've got it all sorted. We'll launch the video first when we're back in England, then later on, when you've had chance to heal, we'll have a big press conference an' stuff. The whole world's gonna hear about the sacrifice yer've made, Karen and it's gonna make folk think."

Karen nodded, squeezing Jude's hand. "Joan of Arc, right?"

"Too right, Joan of fuckin' Arc!" Jude let go of Karen's hand and twisted the ring off her little finger. The silver gargoyle with its garnet eyes winked in the light above the bed. "This… this is for you, Karen. When yer come round from't anaesthetic, it'll be on yer finger, I promise."

"Oh, cheers, Jude – nice one. Only four more to collect and I'll have a knuckleduster like yours!"

A nervous knock, then Yve's head appeared round the door. "They're on their way, two nurses and a doctor." She could feel the door handle fossilising itself into her palm.

Jude bent down and kissed Karen's hand. "Am so proud o'you, our Karen, I can't tell yer. Thank you. Thank you so much."

The two nurses came into the room followed by the anaesthetist. Jude backed towards the door, holding out the ring. "Think on, it'll be on yer finger when yer come round," then she disappeared out into the corridor.

A nurse checked Karen's blood pressure.

"Teck good care o'me down there in the operating room, won't yer," Karen said to the anaesthetist. He smiled and nodded. "And if yer wun't mind, could yer stick the needle in 'ere when yer put me to sleep. That's the 'ole what the last doctor made when I had me appendix out. I'd rather not have another red mark on me hand, if I can help it."

The doctor smiled and nodded again.

"You an't understood a soddin' word I've said, have yer. Christ, s'like pushin' a rope talking to Johnny Foreigner." The two nurses wheeled the bed towards the door. "If I wake up an' find yer've amputated me arm by mistake, I'll not be surprised." Karen laughed. "Bring back the soddin' NHS, eh, all is forgiven."

Chapter M

…a morbid preoccupation with appearance, causing psychological distress that impairs occupational and/or social functioning, and carrying a high risk of suicide…

Am on the computer. First time in… well since it all blew up, really. Or maybe I have been on since. Anyway, am in me room. Been in me room a few days now, weeks, a month. I can't remember. Walls, ceiling, doors – s'all mirrors now. Happy as Larry I am in 'ere though. Wan't all that bothered about going out anyway. Am sat on the floor. Sat on the floor, naked. S'not cold though. Laptop's keepin' me warm. S'like a walter hottle bottle. Gran calls 'em that, don't yer Gran. Walter hottle bottles. She'll not answer. She's downstairs, so she'll not've heard me.

Am online, Wikipedia open on one tab, YouTube on't other. Am flickin' between 'em. On the video, the doctor's just broke me nose. Cun't watch that bit. Am flickin' between the two so I don't have to watch the gory bits. Dun't hurt to watch or owt, cos yer forget the pain, don't yer. Physical pain, I mean. That's why lasses keep on having babies, in't it, even though the first one hurt like buggery. Clever in't it, how yer body dun't remember pain. Physical pain, I mean. Emotional pain - s'a different kettle o'fish, that is. When someone yer trust betrays yer, yer don't forget that kind o'pain. When someone yer cared about uses yer, an' tries to get one over on yer. When someone who should love yer, sods off an' leaves yer, yer don't forget that kind o'pain. That wrenching feeling yer get in yer guts. That feeling of someone stabbing a fork through yer heart an' twisting it round in yer soddin' chest. Yer don't forget that. Been a fork in me chest for days now, weeks, a month. I can't…

…*generally diagnosed in those who are extremely critical of their physique or self-image, even though there may be no noticeable disfigurement or defect…*

Dun't hurt to watch or owt. Yer forget the pain, don't yer. Physical pain, I mean. Them two weeks convalescing in Bucharest after I come out of hospital, I've forgot that pain. Remember it hurting an' that, but I can't remember the pain itself. S'funny that in't it. Clever really, yer body when yer think about it. Means yer can keep on doing stuff to it.

Doctor's just drawn a line of blood round me ear with his scalpel. I trace along the scar with me finger. Just a little bit harder, me nail at a different angle an' the skin'd come away, curl round me finger end like butter.

…*sufferers, generally of normal or even highly attractive appearance, believe they are so unspeakably hideous that they are unable to interact with others, or function normally for fear of ridicule and humiliation about the way they look…*

S'dark in the room. Just the light from me laptop making me chest and legs glow. I like the light. Like how it feels on yer skin an' that. I look across the room an' see me sitting 'ere, all spectral. Ghostly. S'all mirrors now – walls, ceiling, doors. Behind me's the picture I made earlier. S'another composite. One o'me cut-ups. I look at the floor. Newspapers, big holes cut out of 'em. Newspapers telling tales. Resolution. Exoneration. Absolution. Tales with big holes in 'em.

…often misunderstood as a vanity-driven obsession, whereas it is quite the opposite, sufferers believing themselves to be irrevocably ugly or defective…

Swirling a hand in the dry pool of newsprint next to me, I shake me head. They an't got a clue, them journalists. Not about me anyway. They don't know owt, cos I've kept schtum, all this time. They only know what they 'eard on the tape machine, an' what Jude's told 'em. And she dun't know owt, not really. Not what am like, where I live, nobody does. Made sure o'that. Like to keep meself to meself. Allus have. Prefer me own company to other folk's. Things allus get messy round other folk. I get messy.

Doctor's cutting along me right eyelid now. I watch the line bulge red, the red run towards me eyelashes. Dun't hurt to watch or owt.

…combines obsessive and compulsive aspects; sufferers look at themselves in the mirror or avoid them completely. Typically they think about their appearance for at least one hour a day…

I look across the room an' see me sitting 'ere, all spectral. Ghostly. Behind me's the picture I made earlier. S'another composite. One o'me cut-ups. S'me, cut up. Pictures of me taken at the Cow an' Calf Rocks a few days ago, weeks, a month. I can't… Pictures what they stole off me, anyway. Pictures what I've cut out the newspapers.

"This way, Karen!"

Clicking, flashes, shouting.

"Karen!"

"Over 'ere, love!"

"Look this way!

I've dumped the laptop on the floor. In me hand, the cord from the floor lamp. Am flicking the switch, on, off, on, off. Now yer see me, now yer don't. On, off… The clicking, the flashes, the shouting, the betrayal. On, off, on, off…

Am on me feet now, holding the floor lamp like a battering ram. I can feel the violence in it. The violence it's capable of. *Compulsively looking at themselves in the mirror or avoiding them completely.* Ah, but not battering 'em with a floor lamp though, eh! No. Not beating the crap out of 'em with a battering ram!!

Me breath's outside me chest, sitting on it; a dull weight pressing down. I look round the room, the lamp sweaty in me hands. S'all broken mirrors now – walls, ceiling, doors. S'all broken up in bits. Used to like to see meself reflected round the room, but now broken glass is enough. I chuck what's left of the lamp on the bed, then I catch sight of me laptop. On screen, me being broken up. I crouch down and stab the off button. There. I swallow, gripping me legs, cheek pressed to knees. Yer know what? I reckon being happy with yerself takes guts, and well, am… am just not that brave, really.

As of this minute, I've no past. Karen Backhouse has no history, I've decided. The past belongs to other folk. S'for other folk to say, not me. I belong to now. The 'ere an' now. Before this, there was nothing. I was born 'ere just now, to no parents. I look at the cut-up I made. Me, cut up. It's stuck to what's left o'the glass on the bedroom wall. I feel me hands holding me face, me next face, and I smile. Yeah, I love yer too, Karen.

THE BATTLE OF BARNCLEUTH SQUARE

BY
JOSEPH RIDGWELL

beatthedust press

1

One day, around noon, I woke up in a whorehouse. No, it wasn't a whorehouse, just the crumby bed-sit of a junkie street hooker. For a few moments I was disorientated. It was the last days of the twentieth century.

I couldn't remember much from the night before, but I could remember the hooker. She worked the main Darlinghurst drag. I lived just around the corner and I'd see these girls nearly every day.

"Wanna see a lady?" she'd always ask.

I'd always shake my head.

"I'll get ya one day, Pom," she'd call out behind me.

Well, she'd been true to her word. I'd been got. I studied the small room, one-hob stove, toaster, kettle, a green skirt hanging behind a door, various drug paraphernalia, and not much else. This class of prostitute never makes any money. They are on the game out of sheer desperation. There are no rich johns wanting to marry them or big fat bank accounts, nothing apart from the day to day precariousness of street life.

I staggered from the blanket-less bed, clocked the stains on the mattress, and wondered how many other bums had shagged on it. Then I walked to the toilet and vomited, plenty.

After that I drank some cold water straight from the tap, re-hydration. There was a small transistor radio on a dusty window ledge. It was battery-operated and amazingly had power. I turned it on and Bob Dylan singing *Don't Think Twice*, emerged over the airwaves.

Then I thought about the hooker again, buying the batteries for her little radio, and the image choked me up. I mean, you just don't think of junkie hookers doing any of the banal stuff. You think of them buying condoms, KY jelly, or $20 bags of heroin, but even junkie hookers have to do the practical stuff like tie a shoelace or something.

At some point I checked for my things. My wallet was empty, no surprises there, but my jeans and tee-shirt were missing, which was a surprise. I hunted high and low, but they were indeed gone. I found some old tracksuit bottoms that had press studs all down the sides and put them on. I looked odd, but that hardly mattered. There wasn't any money in the apartment, although I did chance across a wad of Mexican Pesos. I'd been to Mexico and knew they were virtually worthless, but pocketed them anyway.

Then I lay down on the stained bed and waited. Outside the sun was shining brightly. Cars and trucks passed by, some disembodied voices, even a scrap of conversation,

"Deano wanted two feet…"

"Two feet?"

I imagined Deano hobbling around without any feet and chuckled to myself.

Hours passed and it grew dark and I got bored. I figured the girl would come back at some time, but also figured there was more chance of seeing her on the main drag.

I walked out into another hot Sydney night, topless. No one took any notice, a bare-chested man being a common sight, and most Kings Cross regulars walked around barefoot.

I found a Bureau De Change and cashed my wad of stolen pesos. While the puny transaction was conducted the teller studied me with a mixture of disgust and fascination. Jesus, for some people, it's a crime being poor. I made $2.60 on the deal though, just enough to buy a longneck of beer, so I was alright.

I took the long walk to the botanical gardens holding my bottle of beer in a brown paper bag. I sat on a bench and watched the ducks and sipped my beer, slowly. The ducks didn't do much, just swam, quacked, ate; mostly they just ate. Occasionally one would chase another and there would be much quacking and splashing. I figured it was easier being a duck than a human being.

I walked back to the main drag. It was quiet, a strange time. I clocked the hooker outside Hungry Jacks. She was wearing my jeans and tee-shirt. The tee-shirt had a picture of a gigantic glass of beer sandwiched between a couple of surfers, with the words, *Journey for the Endless Schooner* printed underneath. I liked that tee-shirt.

As I approached the girl turned her back,

"Any chance of getting my tee-shirt back, ya can keep the jeans," I said.

The girl looked over her shoulder and gave me the once over. I was still topless.

"Fuck Pom, I would but I've got nothing on underneath."

Then the girl turned around and flashed her tits to prove it was true. It was.

I saw the brown nipples on an alabaster backdrop and felt a tiny tingle in the groin region.

"Ah, fuck it, keep the tee-shirt," I replied.

"I'll gives it back to ya, when I sees ya again."

I laughed at that and smiled, then the girl took me completely by surprise. A look of total vulnerability appeared in her vivid green eyes and she bit her bottom lip.

"Hey, why don't cha come back to mine tonight, gets ya tee-shirt back?"

"I'm broke."

The girl smiled awkwardly.

"No, I's mean as mates."

I nearly fainted right there on the sidewalk, but the girl was a train wreck, and I wasn't in much better condition. It was an impossible suggestion, crazy. I started walking backwards and in an instant the girl's hard junkie street hooker, fuck 'em all look returned.

"Na, I can't," I mumbled.

Then I sensed it coming, the retort,

"Go fuck yourself then, ya fuck-up."

Queensland Suzie

Queensland Suzie was the ugliest woman I'd ever seen. Her people were the Guugu Yimithirr and her country was Queensland. Despite being blacker than the ace of spades, Suzie was mixed-race, and that was why she had become one of the Stolen Generation. The authorities tore her from her mother's arms in 1964. This was how Suzie eloquently put it:

"I was with my mum and auntie. They put us in the police ute and said they were taking us to Brisbane. They put the mums in there as well. But as soon as we turned the first corner they stopped, and threw the mothers out of the car. We jumped on our mothers' backs, crying, trying not to be left behind. But the policemen pulled us off and threw us back in the car. They pushed the mothers away and drove off, while our mothers were chasing the car, running and crying after us. We were screaming in the back of that car. We were only six years old. I never saw my mother again."

The Stolen Generation plan was like something out of Nazi Germany. The demented authorities wanted to make all aboriginal people white. When I asked Suzie if she wanted to become white she told me this:

"No's I never did, a? I took one look at the whiteys and how miserable they all were and decided I liked my paint job."

Suzie was a funny girl, and the most loyal and golden-hearted person I ever met. Her weakness was the grog and deadbeat men. Suzie liked a drink and made some terrible choices in members of the opposite sex.

The men in her life were all losers and drunks, wife beaters and punks. None of them stuck around or provided any support. Three children came into the world and were all taken away. Tragic and nearly out of her mind, Suzie somehow made it all the way to Sydney, and the booze-drenched streets of Kings Cross. It was 1999 when I met her and despite everything, the ordeals and travails, this wonder woman was still smiling. I knew I'd never forget her.........

2

It was another hot night in Kings Cross, Sydney. Hot in the city, and somehow a strange notion that everything was going to end, that maybe the millennium might just herald the commencement of the apocalypse, dominated all my evening song thoughts.

These bad omens followed me as I slipped through an oddly deserted Barncleuth Square, and headed down towards Elizabeth Bay and the marina. Rushcutters Park was empty, but I kept my eyes peeled for any police or sticky beaks lurking around. My roll was safely tucked away in a darkened corner of the main spectator stand of the cricket club. I'd been dossing there for the last few days, but another weekend of cricket was just around the corner and pretty soon I'd have to find new digs.

Still, it was a pretty cool place to doss, view of the harbour waters, cool breezes, and on clear nights such as this, starry skies and even a Li Po moon shining down on me. All I needed was a cask of wine and a tent made by the master tentmaker himself, Omar Khayyam. And where was a beautiful woman when you needed one?

Often, in the mornings, I'd smoke a cigarette, gaze at the sparkling harbour waters and beautiful sunshine, think about all the fools at work, and feel well off. There was also a public toilet with shower facilities nearby, so I could even keep myself clean. Ah, the salad days of the romantic bum.

But nothing good lasts forever and I was running out of cash. I stuck a hand into my roll and took out my battered wallet. There were ten fifties inside, the last of my earnings from a few months' work as a dishwasher in a nearby hospital. I fingered the notes and wondered. Yep, there was no doubt about it; I would have to find a job, but 500 bucks gave me a breathing space. I found an old wife-beater vest and slipped it on. Then I found the stub of a cigarette and lit up. I took a few puffs and stared into space. A few dark clouds raced across a midnight blue sky. Suddenly I wanted to be a cloud, nothing to do, but roll about heaven all day long. Or maybe I could just spend my days wandering the earth, from here to eternity.

That was my problem, I was a dreamer, somebody unable or unwilling to adapt to the rigours of modern living. Then there were the others, the other people. I just didn't understand them, the way they looked, walked, talked, their hatred, love, pain, suffering, jealously - I didn't understand any of it. All I wanted to do was drift away.

I rummaged around inside my roll until I located my notepad and pen. Then I attempted to write another pome. Half an hour later I had something, it wasn't much, but there were a couple of decent lines. I'd have to work on it, but it was a promising start. It was the reason I'd come to Australia in the first place. To write poetry, to live the life of a poet as best I could, and be true to some obscure poetical ideal. I thought of Byron, Keats and Shelley. I thought of Rimbaud and Baudelaire. I thought of Li Po and Wei Bai, and then there was Hart Crane and Basho to consider.

Kings Cross, Sydney seemed like a good place to be an aspiring poet. It was the red-light district, home to 24hr bars, strip clubs, and many a bum, junkie and street hooker, down the years. These characters attracted me far more than the so-called successful freaks. I figured I'd write about all those people, immortalise them forever, or something.

I stubbed the butt out, rolled out my dirty sleeping bag and used some jumpers as a pillow. 'Maybe I should've taken the brass up on her offer,' I ruminated as I gazed at the smiling moon and flashing stars. 'I mean, that would've been something.'

Some fruit bats floated past like strange ghosts, and I closed my eyes and slept the sleep of the justified.

Instamatic Camera Lady

She wandered the ragged streets of Kings Cross each and every weekend carrying that incredible camera in her hand. This was back in the days when misfits, drunkards, junkies, street kids, poets, seers and gangsters still roamed the streets of the Cross. The days when the Cross was still inhabited by characters.

And one such character was the diminutive Instamatic Camera Lady. This little old junkie was a sight to behold, dressed like she'd just walked out of a 1940's film noir, and weighed down by what appeared to be the world's first instamatic camera - a strange unwieldy contraption, maybe even a prototype.

And the ancient lady was always immaculately dressed, a vision of style and grace, looking like a wrinkled version of Coco Chanel, or some forgotten movie star of the Hollywood studio era. How she'd survived the years of addiction was a miracle in itself. Somehow avoiding the ODs, lifestyle diseases, and the usual fate of most junkies, to die young or simply fade away.

A born survivor, she appeared on the main drag every weekend, without fail, full make-up on and that absurd camera dangling free. Weaving in and out of every bar, restaurant and café. Propositioning transient revellers with her standard line,

"Would you like your photo taken my lovely? Only five dollars!"

Most people shook their heads, laughed, or simply blanked her, but this indomitable little lady never complained. She just moved on to the next potential punter, until eventually someone drunk enough said,

"Hey yeah, what the fuck, take my photo, grandma."

And hidden away in dusty attics, boxes and cupboards, up and down the country, and maybe all over the world, are little reminders of the old lady. Faded photographs of younger people, long-vanished children and nights, ex boyfriends and girlfriends, husbands and wives, and faded dreams.

And some old-timers in the Cross, relics of a bygone age, insist that if you look very carefully you may be lucky enough to see the old lady, with her oversized camera, gliding along the main drag on a buzzing Saturday night. And if you blink your eyes and look again that old lady might just flash you a grievous smile before whispering hard and low,

"Would you like your photo taken my lovely? Only five dollars!"

3

The next morning I was rudely awakened by the sound of a gruff voice, and something poking into me. I opened my sleep-encrusted eyes and felt the panic. Shit, it was a caretaker of some sort and the fucker was prodding me with a huge broom.

"Alright, alright, take it easy," I mumbled, sleepily.

"What the hell d'ya thinking you're playing at? Ya can't sleep rough in here, mate!" the man growled angrily.

I hurriedly slipped out of my bag and began getting my few paltry things together. As I did, I received two more sharp blows to the ribs.

"Can you stop hitting me with that fucking broom, for fucksakes."

The man continued growling.

"Come on, come on, out, out before I set the dogs on ya."

I hastily stuffed all my things into the roll. The man got me one more time with the broom, a sickening blow to the knee, bang on the funny bone. I saw stars and felt dizzy, but managed to hold it together. I began edging away, along an aisle of empty seats, all the while keeping a close eye on the angry caretaker and his lethal broom.

"What a cunt," I thought, groggily.

The caretaker followed me, broom out front, thrusting and poking like some deranged fencer.

"Your kind always want something for nothing - bloody freeloaders!"

My kind?

"Ok, ok, I'm going. Jesus Christ."

The caretaker stopped advancing and just stood there, high up in the empty spectator stand of the cricket ground, shaking his broom at me like an insane Zen lunatic.

"And don't let me catch you dossing here again or I'll call the police."

Once at a safe distance I stopped, gave the old prick the finger, then spun around and headed back to the main drag, looking for a kiss, or a mystery girl, or better still somewhere to live.

The Radioman

The Radioman was a homeless man, so called because he walked the streets of the Cross with a huge transistor radio strapped to his back. The Radioman liked golden oldies, and his fantastic radio was eternally tuned to hits of yesterday, his favourite track being Crazy by Patsy Cline. Whenever that tune was broadcast, the Radioman would stop what he was doing, fold his arms across his chest, and stand there in the sun burnt streets with a beatific smile on a blissed-out face.

The Radioman originated from South Australia, a descendent of the first Europeans to settle in those parts. Eloquent of speech and dignified in manners, some say the Radioman was as close to Australian aristocracy as anyone in the lucky country could and might ever be..................

4

Just before I got to the main drag, I cut through Barncleuth Square. Crashed out asleep on two dirty mattresses were the Famous Bums, a few empty bottles of port lying forsaken on the dirty ground. Asleep on a bench beside the bums was the drunken Welsh bard, Beermatt. I'd met him a few months before during a brief stay in a nearby hostel, and bumped into him every now and again. Like me, he was an aspiring poet, or that's what he said when I told him I was one, but I'd never seen any evidence of any pomes, not a single one. However, he had come up with one great line:

"All the money disappears into my mouth as the sunlight dims low and merciless across Barncleuth Square."

Maybe he was a one-line poet only.

I pushed his sleeping form.

"Beermatt, get the fuck up."

The bard let out an ungodly groan.

"Ooooohhhhh."

I gave him a judo chop to the ribcage.

"I said up!"

Beermatt shook his head and rubbed his face. Then he eyeballed the longneck beer bottle lying on the ground beneath the bench. He held out a shaky arm, grabbed the bottle, and raised it to his lips. A lone golden droplet fell from the neck of the bottle, catching the sun and sparkling like a mad diamond, before falling onto Beermatt's parched tongue. The alleged poet smacked his lips.

"Fuck it, need a drinnkkk," he croaked. Then he eyeballed me. "Who the fuck are you?"

"Whaddya mean, who the fuck am I?"

Beermatt scrunched up one eye and stared at me again.

"Ah, yeah, Ridgwell. Now what the fuck are you doing here?"

"Got kicked out of the spectator stand at the cricket club. Need a place to crash."

On hearing that Beermatt suddenly jumped up like he'd been electrocuted.

"You're in luck there, my friend," he said mysteriously.

"I am?"

"You are."

"How?"

"You can use my pad for a couple of weeks."

I thought about Beermatt's beat apartment situated in Rat Alley. Small, dirty, cramped, ripped screens, smashed windows, filthy bathroom, and infested with roaches. Put it this way, it was no penthouse, but it had four walls and at that stage in life, I had a theory that all a man needs to survive in the world is four walls. I wondered why the drunken one was offering it to me.

"How comes?"

Beermatt put an arm on my shoulder.

"Come on, let's go get a hair of the dog, and I'll give you the low down."

We walked to the nearest 24hr bar, the *Bourbon and Beefsteak*, and ordered a couple of schooners. Beermatt gulped his down in two large gulps.

"Hit tha spot," he gasped afterwards. "Now listen," he said.

I swigged my Toohey's and listened.

"I'm fucking off."

"Where to?"

"Melbourne."

"Melbourne?"

"Yep, Victoria, gotta a gig lined up working in an apple orchard, harvesting apples - fortnight, three grand, rent-free caravan in the orchard. Nothing to do there, except pick apples and sit outside the caravan and gaze at the stars. Ganna work on my new collection of poetry, earn some cash, and then return to the Cross just before Chrimbo and go on an end of century spree the likes of which the world has never seen."

"Groovy."

"It is, and I'm fucking off now, before this beer buzz wears off. Here's the keys, see ya jus afore the millennium."

And with that Beermatt threw some keys across the beer-spilt counter, walked out of the bar, took a sharp left and disappeared.

I picked up the keys and gazed at them in wonder. Things were looking up.

Bibi the Brazilian Trannie

What he was doing in Sydney, or how he ever made it to those Australian shores from the jungles of South America, we will never know, but make it he did, and all the way to the Cross. The first I knew of him was the sound of his voice, a plaintive lover's call echoing into eternity one sad, hung over Sunday morning. I was lying in bed, beer sick and full of sorrow. I'd over done it again with the vino, gin, and whiskey beer combo, and was suffering. Then the voice, a sad lonesome heartbroken voice, the sound of which I shall never forget.

"Bastardo!"

Repeated over and over.

After a while of this I jumped up and leaned out of the window. And there he was, Bibi the Brazilian trannie in mourning for some long lost lover. And what a vision. Well over six-feet tall, waist length brown hair, smudged lipstick, mascara, ripped top, torn silver mini-skirt and barefoot.

"Bastardo!"

"Bastardo!"

And who was the bastard? Nobody shall ever know.

After that Bibi was regularly found on the corner of William and Victoria, or at the Wall. Plying his trade, whispering offers to "see a lady" to anyone who passed him by. Twosomes, threesomes, gangbangs, it hardly mattered. She was out of it, consumed by drugs and a broken heart, and as everyone knows only love can break your heart.

"Bastardo!"

5

On the way back to my new digs, I cut through Barncleuth Square again. The Famous Bums were still there, but now they were awake and appeared to be in the process of constructing another of their legendary open-air rooms. A wardrobe and a hat stand had appeared alongside the two dirty mattresses.

"How's it going?" I called out as I passed by.

One of the bums, who never spoke, but just growled, did just that, growled at me. I smiled, and the other bum known as Baldie returned my smile.

"We're building a special room for the end of the century, a?" he cackled.

"You are?" I replied.

The bald one grinned somewhat manically.

"Yeep, and we're ganna have all mod cons, go all out for our millennium party."

"Millennium party?"

"Yeep, fack the facking fireworks, mate, and the facking opera house and all that la-di-dah bullshit. All the action be ere in tha Square. You coming Pom?"

"Fucking A."

"That's tha spirit."

A few moments later I stood outside a crumbling Kellett Street Tenement block, key in hand. This was it, The Oakwoods, the building that Beermatt's seedy dive was situated in. I checked for any condemned signs; there were none, an oversight by the civic authorities.

The apartment was on the eighth floor, at the end of a dark and dingy corridor. I snapped on an ancient light switch, and the sound of a million cockroach feet could be heard scurrying into various hidden nooks and crannies.

"Nice," I said aloud.

I stuck the key into a battered door and stepped inside. The outside of Beermatt's place was bad enough, but inside was like a war zone. The dump smelt of stale beer farts, puke, and cigarettes. There was a poky living room, battered settee, empty beer bottles, a radio, a torn poster advertising Bondi beach, a grime-smeared kitchen containing the world's dirtiest cooker, and a decrepit sink filled with dirty dishwater and some broken crockery. However, despite the general state of deprivation, standing in a corner all by itself was a huge 1950's American style fridge.

Amazed, I walked over to the fridge and opened it. Aside from one long neck of beer, the fridge was empty; nothing else in there. It was beautiful. I grabbed the bottle, flipped the cap, and took a swig. It was ice-cold and lush.

The Air-Guitar Man

Make no mistake, it's the characters that give a place its flavour, not business people, council workers, community leaders or mayors. And one such character was the Air-Guitar busker of Kings Cross. This gallant hobo carried all his worldly possessions in two huge red and blue laundry bags, and every now and again dabbled in the lost art of Air-Guitar busking.

He would produce a piece of wood from one of the laundry bags, hold the stick as if it were a guitar and begin strumming. He made no sound, he didn't sing, and he would continue for hours, lost in his own world of silent riffs and noiseless breaks. And if you were foolish enough to toss him a coin, the coin would remain wherever it settled, untouched by the Air-Guitar busker. When finished, he would simply put his stick back inside his bags and walk away. And that, whichever way you look at it, is class, pure class.

6

Once settled into Beermatt's dive, despite the less than salubrious surroundings, I rested easy. All thoughts of apocalypse and the end of the world being nigh, were filtered from the steel wires of my brain and dumped into the waste basket of forgotten memories. My situation was far from secure, but at least I had a roof over my head. Now all I had to do was find some work. Easier said than done, but not beyond the realms of possibility.

The following morning I went out in search of a job. I trawled all the sex shops along the main drag and made some preliminary enquires. Working in a porn shop appealed to my sensibilities. I reckoned on encountering some interesting and seedy characters as I peddled porn. Characters I could write about during lulls in custom in the skin trade. However, I was out of luck. All the positions were filled. It figured - the jobs were mostly cushy numbers.

I wandered up into Oxford Street and Paddington, Sydney's queer quarter. I asked in all the clothes and book shops, cafés, restaurants, but it was the same story as the sex shops. I became disillusioned and fed up, and then my feet began to ache, plus it was hot and I began to sweat from pounding those sun-baked Sydney sidewalks. Then, just as I was about to give up, I saw it, the sign - 'Help Wanted.'

I eyeballed the premises. It was a sandwich and coffee shop, neat, expensive looking, some dull looking coffee addicts sitting at small tables talking shit. Oh well, it was worth a try. I stepped inside and up to the counter.

"I've come about the job," I mumbled to a fresh-faced blonde girl, who was smiling somewhat manically.

Seconds later the owner appeared, a harassed looking, middle-aged woman who possessed a mouth that turned downwards. The upside down visage didn't bode well.

"Come about the job have ya?" she barked.

"Yeah," I replied, languidly.

"Barista?"

Bar-who? "Yep, sort of."

The demented-looking woman, smiled, and her down-turned mouth reversed itself.

"Good, just what we need. Be here tomorrow morning at 7.00 sharp," she beamed.

My job was to work the Expresso machine and serve coffee and tea to leisured faggots, lesbians, and whoever else wandered along Oxford Street during the daytime. When the owner asked if I'd ever used an Expresso machine, I'd lied and said that I had. In reality I'd never been near one in my entire life. And in fact I didn't even drink coffee. I'd always harboured a sneaking feeling that all coffee drinkers possess a fundamental character flaw; they lack passion and energy, and are basically a bunch of stiffs. Whatever. I lied to make sure I got the job, but from the start everything went wrong and the day turned out to be a disaster.

On my arrival the stern-faced owner handed over a dirty old apron and told me to stand in front of the Expresso machine and prepare for the morning rush. Once in position I looked at the machine, wondered what all the buttons, switches, shiny handles, and spouts were for, and panicked. It could have been an alien spacecraft for all I knew. I fiddled with a few knobs and tried to look professional, but it was hopeless, and a sense of impending doom began to consume me.

Shortly after eight, a variety of customers, fairies and dykes dominating, arrived en masse and began ordering coffee with a variety of different names. Immediately I was in trouble.

"Can I have a mocha latte, a short black and a skinny white?" asked a balding middle-aged fading queen, with an, I'm-in-a-rush-so-hurry-up type attitude.

"A skinny what?"

"Can I have two lattes and a camomile and ginger?" demanded an agitated young woman, who was in such a rush I figured she'd just robbed a bank.

"Pardon?"

Due to zero coffee-making skills, I was quickly snowed under, and it wasn't long before I began taking abuse. These coffee drinkers were brutal fuckers, and I was especially taken aback when a pretty girl I'd served a cappuccino consisting of mostly froth and not much else, reacted like this:

"What the hell is this? There's nothing in it, you imbecile."

"Sorry," I replied, humbly.

The girl looked at me like I'd just told her she had a fishy fanny.

"Oh God, I'm going to be late now!"

After that I fiddled around with some cups and jugs and other shit. The start to my new job wasn't going very well, and it quickly became obvious that I wasn't cut out for a career in the coffee-making business.

"We'll make a Barista out of you yet, Pommie," said my overly cheerful and over optimistic co-worker, the blonde with the perm-a-smile. Somehow, I doubted it.

After another customer complaint about one of my dodgy cappuccino's, the owner dragged me away from the machine before I was lynched. If you want to start a revolution just deny all coffee drinkers their morning fix and a million fanatics will be yours.

"I thought you said you'd used an Expresso before, mate?" the owner shouted at me in front of everyone.

'And you can fuck off as well,' I thought angrily.

Next I was stuck on the sandwich counter, but I was nearly as bad at making sandwiches as I was at making coffee. I was sloppy, mixed up orders, dropped fillings on the floor and cut the things unevenly.

In desperation I observed the other assistants. They appeared to know exactly what they were doing. They were quick, efficient, and had an uncanny ability to remain ultra-polite and smile all the time. 'Why can't I be like them?' I ruminated, as I fucked up some more sandwich orders.

When lunch was over the owner took me off the sandwich counter, pointed to a broom and dustpan, and told me to get sweeping. To be demoted twice in one morning was probably some kind of record. As I swept crumbs and dust from the floor in a lazy languid fashion, I realised with a strange loser satisfaction that it was now impossible to go any lower in the hierarchy of the sandwich shop.

After a few half-hearted sweeps of the broom the owner began staring at me. The stares freaked me out, but I pretended not to notice and carried on regardless. A minute later she dashed from behind the counter and rushed up to me.

"That's not how you sweep, fella. Watch and I'll show ya how to do it properly!" she bawled. Then she snatched the broom from my grasp and began sweeping the floor with swift manic strokes. I was impressed.

When the demonstration was over she thrust the broom back into my hands.

"Put some elbow grease into it, Pom," she shrieked.

Unperturbed, I ignored the advice and carried on in exactly the same way. Then, when I considered the job done, I put the dustpan and broom back in their rightful place. The owner shot me a look of disbelief, mixed with a hint of malice.

"Have you finished?"

"Yeah," I replied like I didn't give a fuck, even though I did, but I couldn't help myself.

The owner looked at me strangely like I had spoken in Mandarin or Swahili.

"Okay Pom, hand us ya apron and wait over there by the window."

I handed her the apron and waited over by the window. All the other smiling assistants were still working and I felt like a naughty school kid. The owner kept me waiting for over twenty minutes.

"Sorry about that, Pom. Look here's a day's pay, minus the last two hours." she said as she handed over two crisp twenty-dollar notes. "I don't think we'll need you after today," she added, abruptly.

I walked out of that shop forever. On the way back to Kings Cross I began to feel like a completely useless piece of shit that was no good to anyone. I'd been banking on a full week's pay to keep me going for another fortnight, but forty dollars wasn't even enough to last more than a couple of drinks in Barncleuth Square, let alone all the other essentials of life.

I wandered back to the main drag of Kings Cross in a daze. On the corner of Darlinghurst and Bayswater, I brought a slice of two-dollar pizza from a takeaway outlet and sat down on a bench. I took a large bite of the rubbery pizza slice and wondered how it had come to this. 'How do these fuckers get by?' I asked myself, as several purposeful-looking people walked past.

Despite my earlier optimism, it appeared that I'd hit rock bottom. Then it dawned on me. What did it matter? When it comes right down to it, rock bottom isn't as bad as you might expect. I still felt the same and looked the same. In fact I was the same. I just didn't have any money.

To my left, sat a beggar wrapped up in a thin grey blanket. A grimy hand, clasping a crumpled paper coffee cup stuck out from the middle of the blanket, and from the bottom a pair of dirty toes emerged. Balanced on the toes was a small cardboard sign. The sign read, *'homeless and hungary, plaese help.'*

Every so often a passer-by threw some change into the cup. After observing the vagrant for several minutes, I realised that I had been wrong all along. To survive in Sydney it appeared all I had to do was sit on the floor and hold my hand out in the classic beggar style. What the fuck? I could probably also write poetry about my experiences as a bum. Hobo Tales or Songs of the Beggar.

I continued to observe the vagrant and estimated that in little over an hour he had made around $2.50 in donations. This was enough to buy a 750ml longneck of beer or a burger. 'Not a bad a rate for just sitting on the floor and looking pathetic,' I reasoned intelligently. 'Don't even have to know how to spell.'

The Umbrella Man

Before he became the Umbrella Man, this legendary Sydney vagrant was the proud owner-occupier of the Starlight Hotel.

Ah, let me tell you about the Starlight Hotel, a ramshackle structure made from bits of old wood, cardboard, scrap metal, and from where the Umbrella Man was able to enjoy the best views in Sydney. The Starlight Hotel nestled high on a cliff top above Mrs Maquarie's chair, with uninterrupted views right across Sydney harbour and beyond.

But the inevitable day arrived when a gang of faceless bureaucrats paid a visit to the Starlight Hotel and issued a closure notice. The hotel was dangerous, unsafe, an eyesore that must be shut down. The Umbrella man was heartbroken. This was his home, a home he had built with his own loving hands. He wasn't hurting anyone, just minding his own business and stargazing. But his protests were in vain and the hotel was closed, dismantled, and taken away without a hint of compassion.

It was then that he morphed into the Umbrella Man. From that day on he could be seen walking the sun burnt Sydney streets with several umbrellas strung across his back. At night he would unfold the umbrellas, form them into an improvised tent, and spend the night under their shelter. Whenever the authorities appeared to continue their relentless persecution, he just packed up his umbrellas and moved on, free as a bird, a determined smile on a determined face, going wherever the wind blew.

7

Three days later I still hadn't found any work. Christmas Day came and went. The last days of the century came and went. I didn't even go out. I just stayed in my room avoiding the world. I wasn't writing any poetry. I was just waiting for something to happen. Waiting, waiting, waiting...............

Did I say Christmas day came and went and I didn't go out? Well, that was a lie, for although the day did indeed come and go, I didn't stay in. No, for although I lived like a recluse, I did venture out onto the streets and had an odd little adventure on the day that Jesus Christ was born. Here's what happened.

On the day in question I was alone with nothing to do. And it was hot, very, very, hot. I was sitting in Beermatt's favourite armchair, sweating without moving, watching the mechanical movements of an extended family of roaches. An insect death dance, and in my gloomy frame of mind it was my impending death they were celebrating. It was then that I knew. I had to leave the flat or die.

For Northern Europeans, Southern hemisphere Christmases are a little disorienting. Like where's the snow, the cold winds, long nights, etc. Instead there are endless sunny days, one blue sky after another, and no respite from the heat anywhere. And then there are the sultry, oppressive evenings, balmy evenings, where intermittent murderous thoughts cross your mind, and the only thing to do is drink cold beer in a darkened room and wait for the dawn.

Fuck it, at eleven I decided to go for a swim. There was a plush apartment block nearby with a communal pool, brand spanking new, just been built. Of course it was for residents only, but that wasn't about to put me off. I slung a six-pack of Carlton Cold into a cooler bag and sauntered over.

Dropping my bag over and scaling the big fence, I found myself in a car park. I walked towards the pool like I owned the place. Inside it was deserted, the water of the pool undisturbed, placid, a tranquil scene. Then I saw it, the vision. I pushed my straw hat back on my head and blinked, and yet my eyes had not deceived me. For, get this fellas, sunbathing in a far corner, butt naked was a statuesque platinum blonde. And no she was not lying on her stomach. I know it sounds unbelievable, but it was true.

I found a sun lounger not far from the vision. She had these big white plastic sunglasses on and there was a yellow flower in her hair. It was love at first sight. I was opening one of my chilled bottles when the vision looked up. She did it like this, lifting her sunglasses and shielding her view with a neatly manicured hand to the brow, red nail varnish, pure class. I tried not to look directly at her chest or pussy regions and raised my beer.

"Happy Christmas," I said.

"Hi," replied the girl, languidly. Then she put her sunglasses back on and turned onto her stomach.

She was tanned from head to toe, no white areas. Shit, I thought. I stared at her delectable derriere and a violent urge to take her from behind took a hold of me. I downed a couple of huge swigs of beer to control myself. It was mental torture, that big brown arse smiling at me, the long platinum blonde hair lying to one side of a delicate shoulder blade, even the yellow flower. God, it was pure torture. I swigged my beer and tried to focus on other shit, flowers in a meadow, angels dancing in heaven, but it was useless……

After re-adjusting my shorts, I stared at the still water of the pool, so blue and inviting. Then I knew what needed to be done, I had to do a bomb. I took my hat off, downed my beer, and launched myself into the water, hands clasped across my knees.

When I surfaced the girl was still sunbathing. I swam a few lengths and wondered why she was all alone on Christmas day. Then I began a slow underwater wank, but halted halfway through. What if the vision took a dip just after I'd spurted my wad into the pool, and some of my spermatozoa somehow swam up her pussy and impregnated her? I wasn't sure if this was biologically possible, but decided to err on the side of caution just in case.

Then I found a rubber ring and jumped inside and floated around. I sipped beer in the sun and watched cloud formations. It was Christmas day, Kings Cross, Sydney, in the last days of the millennium. I floated around and around. The blue sky was everywhere, the golden sun, rays of brilliant white. I could hear nothing, but the sound of a cool breeze rustling palm tree fronds. Gradually I fell into a meditative state and my mind became a blank canvas.

When I awoke the vision had disappeared and a man was addressing me, a security guard of some sort. Working on Christmas day?

"Which apartment do you live in, sir?" he fired at me, somewhat aggressively.

"Twenty-seven," I lied.

"Sir, there is no apartment twenty-seven. I must ask you to leave."

Trust my luck. "Ok," I said, simply.

Before leaving I took a glance around. The pool was deserted, the water once more tranquil and still, everyone else visiting relatives or committing suicide. I grabbed my cooler bag.

"Happy Christmas," I said on my way out.

"Happy Christmas," said the security guard.

He wasn't a bad bloke really, just doing his job, I suppose.

I walked along the main drag on the shady side of the street. There was hardly anyone around. Outside Playbirds stood an old Chinese brass. I often saw her. She must have been at least sixty. She was licking a 15 cent McDonald's cone and smiled as I passed.

"Wan see lady, it Chrimbo?" she squawked.

The brass was correct, it was Chrimbo, but that didn't necessarily mean I wanted to see a lady, especially one that decrepit. I shook my head and walked on.

At the El Alamein fountain I got talking to a couple of well-known bums, the Radioman and Queensland Suzie. They mentioned the outdoor room that the two Famous Bums had been constructing in Barncleuth Square. They reckoned it was their best ever and would never be surpassed. Intrigued, we took a mosey on down to check things out.

Queensland Suzie and the Radioman were right, the room was impressive. The Famous Bums had really gone to town. The finest incarnation of their endless series of open-air rooms, consisted of four settees, three armchairs, seven double mattresses, a painting hanging lopsided from a branch of a tree, a working radio that was on, but not tuned into a station, two televisions (not working), a large blue china vase with some dead flowers in, a wardrobe, coffee table, a broken fridge and freezer, even a hat stand.

The amazing room had attracted an assortment of bums who regularly inhabited the Cross, and a boozy outdoor party was in full swing. Aside from me, Queensland Suzie and the Radioman, the Air-Guitar Man was there, Junkie Pete, Bibi the Brazilian Trannie, The Instamatic Camera Lady, a few other assorted nobodies, and miscellaneous mangy pets. They were all drinking port wine and living it up.

I said hi and strolled around the room. I tried to tune the radio without success. The Famous Bums were in their element and really proud of their achievement. They kept talking about settling down and never moving on again. I began to worry. Under normal conditions their open-air rooms only lasted a few days. After that the authorities moved in for dispersal with clinical efficiency. Maybe because of the festive season they were giving the bums a bit of leeway, but I reckoned it was bound to end in tears.

I drank the last of my beers and brought some more, two longnecks, and a cask of wine for Queensland Suzie.

As we sat drinking and talking shit, I could see the old Chinese brass standing outside Playbirds International. A vision of the platinum blonde kept flashing before my eyes and I began to feel horny. Eventually I strolled over.

"Wanna see a lady?" cackled the ancient brass.

"Let's go," I said.

Chinese hired a $10 room above Porkies Adult Bookshop, which I paid for. There was a black vinyl bench inside the room. I got up on the bench and dropped my shorts, but kept my straw hat on.

"Wha you wan?"

"How much for a hand job?"

"Fifteen dollar."

Bargain, I thought and nodded.

The old chink pulled out several tissues and wrapped them around my penis. What the fuck? Did she go through this rigmarole with every client, or did I look diseased? Maybe it was the straw hat.

The brass got into a rhythm and I closed my eyes and thought of the platinum blonde. It didn't take long, even with the tissues, but just before I came, the old chink became excited and stuck a hand inside her panties.

"Young boy, you jus young boy, young boy," she moaned.

Then she did a strange thing, a thing I will always remember. She licked up all my wad, giving the head of my penis a thorough cleansing. I looked at her in amazement.

"Protein," she said by way of explanation.

Freaky shit.

Outside, aside from a party of amateur drunks, the streets were deserted. It was still Christmas day. I brought another couple of longnecks and returned to the fountain. Queensland Suzie and the Radioman had disappeared and it was beginning to get dark. The old Chinese brass was still standing guard outside Playbirds International, eating another 15 cent McDonald's cone, and lapping up the cream in exactly the same way she had lapped up my cum.

Candice

I first saw Candice on the main drag standing outside Crazy Prices. And it was the eyes that captured my imagination, ocean blue, and beautiful. This was one week before Christmas 1999. I was sitting on a bench outside O'Malley's, 4am, Sunday morning. Then I saw her, Candice, aboriginal, mad hair, big white necklace, flimsy see-through yellow blouse and purple satin trousers. Items so sad and pitiful I could have burst into tears just looking at them. She sat next to me on the bench. She was high, she was fucked, she offered herself for fifty dollars. But none of that mattered, what mattered were the eyes, those blue and damned forever eyes. Eyes I would never get over.

      The next time I saw Candice I asked her to run away with me, and she said yes. She said yes, but in the hard light of another hung-over morn, the girl who said yes had vanished into the sunrise and I never saw her again..................

8

The day before New Years Eve I was plotted up in Beermatt's grimy Kellett Street apartment wondering when something might happen. Aside from my Christmas day expedition, and a few visits to the nearest bottle shop, I had remained holed up inside the beat apartment for the duration. My financial situation was getting perilous; I was down to my last $300. I gazed out of a window and wondered whether to jump, when the sight of a drunken man disturbed my suicidal equilibrium.

Instantly I recognised the swaying figure as that of the alleged poet Beermatt, he who had generously allowed me to stay in his beat apartment for free. Although I was glad to see him, I was also worried that he might ask me to move out. Then I would be well and truly fucked. The streets were getting closer.

After watching Beermatt's drunken meanderings for a while, I called down.

"Dude, where the fuck youse going?"

At that the drunken poet stared in the direction of his own apartment like an old chicken. I waved him up.

"Aye, yey, with the power of ten tigers!" he roared loud enough for the whole fucking city to hear.

Power of ten tigers? What the fuck?

An age later Beermatt finally made it up the eight flights of stairs. I was sitting in the living room with the lights off.

"Youse won't believe what's happened to us," he slurred, as soon as he crossed the threshold.

I eyeballed the drunken poet. There was something odd about him, but at first I couldn't put my finger on it. Luckily, I'd just re-stocked the 1950's American fridge. "Drink?" I offered.

Beermatt collapsed onto a battered settee and nodded.

After returning with the beers I clocked the ears and suddenly recognised the Star Trek connection. "What's with the Spock ears?"

Beermatt touched the latex rubber covering his real ears and smiled.

"Ah, yeah, what d'ya reckon, freaky a?"

"Negative Captain," I replied lamely.

"Put 'em on," he grunted.

I put the Spock ears on without protest and then pointed the finger. "So what the fuck did happen to you?"

With that Beermatt told me the whole sorry, drunken tale. It took a while and he repeated several sections, several times, but this was the short and tall of it. He'd gone to the apple orchard in Victoria as planned, but only lasted four days on the gig before he was bitten by a snake.

"Bitten by a what?"

"A mother-fucking python, hiding in one of the mother fucking apple trees!"

"Jesus Christ."

"Still, I managed to get two grand out of it."

"You did?"

"I did. Told the farmers I was ganna sue their arse, and the freaked fuckers paid me off. Mind you I could've died, a?"

I flipped the cap off my bottle and took a hit. "Tell me everything."

Beermatt flipped the cap off his bottle. "This is how it all went down. There I was, picking apples in the early morning sun, composing sonnets, proper immortal pomes and shit in my head when I saw it."

"Saw what?"

"The snake. It was massive, biggest snake I've ever seen, like a fucking Godzilla of snakes, or you know like that film Anaconda?"

"So a big motherfucker, then?"

"Yeah, but it looked dead. No, it was dead. So I thought might as well pick it up, but when I did the fucker only came alive and bit me on the arm!"

"Jesus Christ."

Beermatt showed me the wound, two small dots, unimpressive. The reptile had only been dozing, warming its cold reptilian blood in the early morning sun. Beermatt continued in the same melodramatic vein.

"Had to spend two days in the local hospital, at death's door, life hanging in the balance. Then the media came a sniffing and the owners of the orchard shit themselves. They appeared incredibly paranoid about any negative publicity. That's when they made the offer."

"The offer?"

Beermatt smiled somewhat evilly. "Yeah, the offer to take the money and go quietly."

"And you took it?"

Beermatt pulled out a thin wad of dollars from his pocket and waved them in the air. "Yeah, fuck it. I mean, I was ok, and I figured two thou was enough corn for my end of century spree."

"Blinding."

"It is, but you know what?"

"What?"

"It's taken me four days to get back to Sydney."

"Four days? How?"

"Fell asleep on the bus just before Parramatta."

"And?"

Beermatt looked at me with those big heavy-lidded eyes of his, eyes that somehow seemed to contain all the suffering and sadness in the world.

"And the bus took me all the way back to Melbourne. Woke up just outside Albury."

"So what happened next?"

Beermatt held out his hands. "Nothing else for it, but have a couple of schooners in the nearest rub-a-dub."

I nodded in empathy. "Understandable, and then you caught the next bus to Sydney?"

Beermatt gave me the inevitable lost stanza look with the eyes once more. "Na, I got blind, but managed to jump on the last bus out of town. Fucking only fell asleep again."

"And no one woke you up at Sydney?"

"Woke up just outside Albury!"

After that convoluted story of catastrophe and woe we stayed up drinking late into the night. At some point Beermatt became delirious and began talking about the power of ten tigers and other meaningless shit. I put it down to the effects of the snake bite-booze combo, and feared for his sanity.

The poet passed out on his booze- and cigarette-burnt sofa around 4am. I put a coat over him to keep him warm. Then I looked out of the window and stared at an empty street. All was quiet, nothing stirred, and the streetlights glowed yellow and luminous.

At some point, a group of young people emerged from a nightclub, shattering the frozen tranquillity. As they approached the apartments I began to discern some individual characteristics - a fat arse, big nose, even a mole.

A brown haired girl skipped along in the middle of the street. She looked up. I was still wearing the Spock ears and drinking my beer.

"Having a beer?" she cried.

"Yeah," I replied, grinning maniacally.

A half-smile formed on the girl's mouth, then she saw the ears, registered them, and instantly the smile disappeared. I put the beer on the windowsill, placed my arms akimbo, screwed up my eyes, and poked out my tongue. Horrified, the girl put a hand to her mouth, spun around, and ran back to her friends.

"I possess the power of ten tigers," I screeched into the approaching dawn and the commencement of another fucked up day of death.

After that I chucked the Dr Spock ears to the floor and tried to work out where I was. It was 6am and the sun had already risen in the east like a thief. I shuffled into Beermatt's bedroom and collapsed onto his spunk-stained mattress, sparko. Tomorrow it would be New Years Eve 1999.

Famous Bum #1 Growler

In all the time I knew him the Growler never uttered an intelligible word. That was why he was called the Growler. He just growled all day long, that's what he did. And along with Baldie, his partner in crime, he was the main architect and constructor of the seemingly never-ending series of open-air rooms that made both of them famous. And there is something to be said for that. The rooms were situated all over the Cross, Bayswater, William, Victoria, Darlinghurst, Orwell, McLeay, Roslyn, Ward, Kellett, and last but not least, The Great Room of Barncleuth Square. Of course that was in the last days of the twentieth century and nothing like that has ever been seen again in the Cross. And where the Growler came from, or where he finally went is a mystery, but to those in the know, to those who were witness to his vagrant nobility and incomprehensible jargon, all are agreed that the likes of him will never be seen again............

9

As the run-up to the end of the century continued, the major news item, aside from the usual death, wars, pestilence, disease and famine shit, was something called the Millennium Bug. According to all the so-called expert commentators and scientists, this Bug was to be the end of civilisation as we knew it, causing all the world's computers to malfunction.

    In fact the media were sending out so many panic signals, me and Beermatt began to wonder if the first human being had walked the earth with a PC strapped to his backside. It was total bullshit, but it sold a few newspapers and increased viewing figures. Life went on.

But, strangely, the people began to get worried. Fundamentally, despite the fact that most were living piss shit turd lives filled with banal misery, they were afraid of dying. Opportunists published best selling books on how to survive the impending catastrophe, and people began stocking up on essential items such as bottled water and tinned food. Some extremists even constructed nuclear bunkers.

Me and Beermatt watched TV reports of people forming queues to buy emergency supplies, in a totally indifferent manner, and even when the supermarket shelves began to empty we remained unconcerned. Our only worry was that the beer might run out, and then we really would have a crisis on our hands. A city without alcohol was a doomsday scenario; a pub without beer too awful a vision to contemplate. Eventually we succumbed to the general sense of hysteria.

So, on News Years Eve, Beermatt went out early to purchase some emergency supplies of our own. "Just in case the panic signals are actually true," he told me with a wink, as he stepped out into another blinding white Sydney summer's day. "Plus, I need a hair of the dog."

At noon Beermatt hadn't returned and, fearing for his safety, I decided to go out onto the streets and search for him. Actually I wasn't really worried, but a sudden urge to see what was happening outside overwhelmed me, plus I also wanted a drink. Beermatt's apartment was situated in the middle of a street of brothels, and on passing Simone's Club for Gentlemen, I decided to pop inside.

At that time of day, Simone's was quiet and I spent an enjoyable hour or two chatting to the girls and resisting all requests to fuck my brains out, suck me dry, etc. I forgot all about Beermatt.

Then, just as I was thinking of leaving, Beermatt popped his head in. He was already half-pissed. "Knew I'd find you in here. What you up to tonight?" he said with a wink and a nudge.

It was then that it dawned on me. I hadn't made any plans for the biggest night of the cock-sucking century. "Fuck knows."

Beermatt shot me another boozy wink. "I've pulled two Dutch sorts and they want me, I mean us, to take them on a guided tour of Sydney. You know strip club, pokies, bars, then later on the fireworks."

Despite the fact that the world was about to end and people were dying in the streets and committing suicide in lonely apartments dotted across the city, the mayor of Sydney had spent over a million bucks on a massive fireworks' display. Well, if it was going to be the end of the world, at least it would be ending in Technicolor. I said goodbye to Simone's lovely ladies, drained my beer, and hit the afternoon end of century streets.

Outside were two young blonde girls, tall, blue-eyed and incredibly pretty. I wondered how Beermatt did it.

"Hi, my names Elsa," said the first Dutch girl.

"Hi, I'm Inga," said the second.

After intros we went straight to the nearest bar. I bought the first round and then Beermatt began bullshitting on a massive scale. Apparently his parents owned land and property all over the UK, and were sailing out from Europe to meet him in their ocean-going yacht. I wasn't impressed, but the girls were.

After the bar we went to an expensive seafood restaurant in Darling harbour. With the two thousand burning a hole in his pocket, Beermatt was generous enough to pay for everything. Now the girls were really impressed, especially when I made sure to order a couple of bottles of quality champagne to go with our delicious dinner.

Once the meal was over, it was time to head to the fireworks' display. After the bubbly and fine food, we were all in good spirits, all except Beermatt who suddenly began to look the worse for wear. I wondered vaguely if it had anything to do with the snake-bite he got in the apple orchard in Victoria.

We found a good observation point in a park overlooking Elizabeth Bay. The harbour bridge was in full view. There were crowds of people everywhere and the people were in the mood to party like they'd never partied before. It was the end of the century, the end of a thousand years of history, and everyone appeared loose-limbed and animated. Expectancy hung in the air like a trapeze artist, and the millennium good vibrations resounded into the night like a gigantic invisible comfort blanket.

Meanwhile, Beermatt was continuing to talk bollocks. I listened in. Apparently he was going to invest in lucrative uranium and plutonium mines in Western Australia, and then fossick for opals. Once he had made his fortune, or several fortunes, he was going to become an international playboy. The girls didn't seem as impressed as before and when he pissed up a tree in full view of everyone, including families with children, they began to distance themselves.

As we stood there waiting for midnight, a wave of anxiety washed over me. I suddenly realised we didn't have any alcohol, and I began to panic. There were four six-packs in the fridge of Beermatt's apartment. I sized up the two girls, trying to work out which one might be up for a shag. Eventually I decided it was the smaller of the two, Inga. She was drunk and had been laughing at all my really lame jokes, the same one's I tell to all new girls I meet.

I popped the question.

"We both come," said Elsa.

I had to think on my feet. Beermatt was swaying and closing his eyes.

"Inga, why don't you come with me, while Elsa keeps an eye on Beermatt," I stated casually.

Immediately Inga was up for it and her enthusiasm impressed me. Elsa looked at Beermatt and frowned. "Okay, just don't be long," she warned.

Once in Beermatt's filthy apartment I jumped on the settee and put my feet up. Inga remained in the doorway, looking at the flat like it was infected with an incurable and incredibly infectious disease,

"Shouldn't we be getting the beer?" she asked.

I jumped up and bundled her into the apartment. "Fuck the beer and come over here, Miss Amsterdam."

Inga let out a peal of nervous laughter. "I'm not from Amsterdam."

I grabbed her head and began kissing her violently. When she responded I didn't fuck around. I began tearing off her clothes, along with mine. Soon I was naked and she was down to her bra and knickers. It was then that she tried to stop me.

"No, no, what are you doing?"

"Fucking you, that's what I'm doing, the last fuck of the century." Then I ripped off her bra and began taking alternative bites on each pink nipple.

"Ohh, argh, oh my god, you are raping me!"

I stuck a hand into her pussy. It was wet. Very, very wet, like a Bangladeshi flood region or the Mekong Delta. I manoeuvred into position. "You want it as much as me," I grunted.

Inga looked me in the eye, like an animal caught in the headlights, doomed, but still alive. "No, stop, this is rape."

Just as I was wondering if it was rape, I suddenly slid all the way in. Inga groaned, said something in Dutch, and then stuck her tongue down my throat.

When it was over I jumped up. "We'd better get back to the others."

Inga was lying on my settee, naked, stroking one thigh and holding a hand to her mouth. She looked like a Rembrandt painting. "You raped me," she whispered.

I chucked her clothes at her. "Stop being dramatic, that wasn't rape, it was a memorable experience, one that will linger long in the memory." Then I grabbed three six packs of beer and chucked them into an eskie.

By the time we got to the park, the fireworks had already began. Beermatt was lying on the grass fast asleep and Elsa was sitting on the harbour wall with a face like a cat's arse.

"Where the hell have you been?" she fired accusingly.

I went to start bullshitting, but Inga beat me to it. "Look at the fireworks, aren't they beautiful?"

All three of us stared at the fireworks. The night sky was filled with dazzling colour and light. People cheered, champagne corks popped and fizzed. It really was the end of the century. Shortly after midnight, people began leaving the park in droves. I kicked Beermatt in the gut. He had slept through the whole thing.

Beermatt jumped up and eyeballed us. "Come on people, the night is young." he croaked.

"We shall return to the hostel," said Elsa resolutely.

Beermatt raised his eyebrows. "Are you nuts? This is the millennium, the beginning of a new century, we will never witness the likes of this again!"

Elsa began walking away. "Come on Inga."

Beermatt held out his hands. "Don't you want us to walk you back to the hostel?"

"Don't bother, we know the way."

Before leaving Inga gave me a peck on the cheek. "Will I see you again, I might be carrying your baby," she whispered.

I took this freaky comment in my stride. "Got a pen?"

She found a pen and a scrap of paper, and I wrote an imaginary telephone number down. "Call me."

Once the girls had disappeared Beermatt and me worked our way back to the Cross. The city was like a war zone, stragglers and casualties of the merriment spread out everywhere. There was a free concert in the domain, a sixteen-piece Cuban band playing a loud, infectious rumba.

It was late by this time and the first hint of dawn had already begun to appear. Then a sea mist descended from out of nowhere and gave everything - buildings, people - a ghost-like appearance. Maybe it really was the end of the world.

Somehow I lost Beermatt in the mist. Then I was alone. I found myself outside the Sydney Opera House at the coming of the dawn. At sunrise, two aboriginal didgeridoo players and a lone blonde girl appeared high up on a ledge of the architectural oddity.

The girl began singing the Australian national anthem and the aboriginal men blasted their wooden pipes. It was a haunting, but beautiful scene and suddenly I experienced an epiphany. I was never going to be a poet and I was never going to return to the UK. I was going to wander Australia, from one place to another for a period of five years like the hero of a Henry Lawson story.

I would become an observer of the Australian people and landscapes - city, bush, and outback. Then, when my wanderings were over, I would write my opus. A two thousand page tome about the lucky country, simply entitled, *Australia, A Journey*. It would be a labour of love, the first great Australian novel ever written, and would ensure my immortality. I sat on some steps and took it all in, the beginning of a new career, the beginning of a new millennium, the start of a new century, the end of the world.

I listened to the mysterious sounds of the didgeridoos and closed my eyes. When I awoke the girl and aboriginal men had disappeared, and I was surrounded on all sides by inane tourists babbling away and taking insane amounts of photographs. I stood up, forgot all about my epiphany, and headed back to the Cross

On my return, the streets were empty and oddly desolate. Litter and rubbish lay strewn everywhere, the aftermath. As I passed Simone's Club for Gentlemen I stepped inside. The place was as empty as the streets outside, the Marie Celeste of brothels.

I plopped myself down on a bar stool. "Anyone in?" I hissed.

The owner appeared, a fat middle-aged woman with masses of grey hair and a gigantic mole on her left cheek. "Jesus mate, you look like shit."

"I feel like shit."

"All the girls have gone home, bud, it's New Year's day."

"Don't I know it. Any chance of a beer?"

The Madame smiled tenderly. "Here, have one on the house, a?"

I took the bottle of VB. "Cheers. Hey, is your computer working?"

"Yeah, why?"

"Thought so," I said, and took a big swig of beer, which didn't go down very well.

Famous Bum #2 Baldie

Baldie was the partner of the Growler and the two dipsomaniacs were inseparable; one rarely seen without the other. There were even those who went so as far as to say they were lovers. Of course this cannot be proven, but often, after a heavy day's drinking, the inebriated pair could be found wrapped in each others arms on a dirty mattress in the last years of the twentieth century.

Baldie was a tall man, well over six-foot, rangy, and as bald as a coot. He suffered terribly from acute psoriasis and the mange, his feet being particularly afflicted and troublesome. How Baldie got together with the Growler is unknown, but their shared love of the grape and outdoor room construction, enabled them to become famous to those in the know. Of South Australian origin with distant Scottish roots, it is said that Baldie migrated to the grimy back streets of the Cross after a failed marriage and the collapse of a pizza delivery business. His favourite tipple was dirt cheap and sweet-tasting fortified wine, which he drank by the litre.

10

A day after New Year's I was standing outside the Pink Pussycat, swigging a longneck of VB from a brown paper bag, and observing the new century scenes. It was the noughties, all the computers were working, and Beermatt was still on the missing list. I figured he had drowned in the harbour. Then Queensland Suzie walked past.

"Yo Suze, what's up?"

To say Suzie was an ugly woman would be a little cruel, but it has to be said she was the ugliest women I'd ever seen. The first time I met her I'd been struggling to pick up this aristocratic English girl from the pavement. I'd met the Marchioness of Jute in the *Bourbon & Beefsteak* and she'd consumed a little too much of the traditional Sunday 2-4-1 vino. After chatting her up all afternoon, I thought I was in like Flynn, but as we staggered outside the bar together, she collapsed on the main drag puking claret everywhere. She wasn't a big girl, but drunk she was a dead weight, and I just couldn't get her up. Plus I didn't fancy any red stains on my favourite *Journey for the Endless Schooner* tee-shirt.

Queensland Suzie was sitting outside Crazy Prices, watching my feebleness with some amusement. "You're as weak as shit, mate," she said after my fourth failed attempt. I remember looking up and seeing this very dark and very ugly aboriginal woman.

"Couldn't give us a hand could ya?"

"Fuck that shit, a?"

"Nice."

And that was that, she didn't give me a hand, and I was forced to leave the Marchioness lying in the gutter. Anyway, for what its worth, that was how I first met Queensland Suzie.

"'appy New Year, Pom. Coming to the square to get boozy with Baldie an Growler?"

Baldie and Growler, nicknames for the two Famous Bums, who built the open-air rooms in Barncleuth Square. The mystery was that nobody knew their real names.

"Is Beermatt there?"

Suzie nodded. "Yeah."

"You mean he didn't drown in the harbour?"

"Huh?"

"Forget it, let's go."

When I got to Barncleuth Square, my eyes nearly popped out of my head. The room was now several rooms, with make-shift walls, some tents, and a couple of doors. It looked like some debauched and defunct Arabian caravan that had got lost on some long forgotten dusty road to Damascus, and then had somehow ended up in the land of the never never. I was impressed.

Along with the ordinary bums and alki's were an assortment of revellers, buskers, teeny-bopper junkies, tourists, backpackers, and just some people who looked lost. I wandered the rooms until I caught sight of Beermatt. He was seated between two broken alki birds, engaged in some in-depth convo. The women were about as fucked up as you could get, and pissed as newts. I spotted the bottle of port in Beermatt's hand, figured he was looking at the broken women through the eye of the grape, and bowled over.

"What's up?" I fired at them.

Beermatt looked up at me out of a pair of bloodshot eyes. He raised the bottle of gut-rot port he was drinking. "Hey, hey Ridgwell, you're alive."

"What d'ya mean, I'm alive?"

Beermatt took a hit of the vino. "Figured you'd drowned in the harbour."

Figured I'd drowned in the harbour? "Huh?"

"Yeah, was just telling these lovely ladies here of your tragic demise."

Lovely ladies? I eyeballed the women. "Did he?"

"Yeah," said one of the scrags. "He said we had to commiserate him because his best friend was dead."

I leaned over and took the bottle from Beermatt's hand and squashed myself in-between him and one of the lovely ladies. "Fuck it, might as well drink to my memory then."

11

We partied hard that final night, everyone drunk and drugged on the most hardcore millennium spree to end all sprees. It was lucky we even survived. I matched Beermatt drink for drink, and we wandered from room to room, talking to everybody and anybody.

Sometime towards dawn I found myself sprawled on an armchair next to a beautiful teenage aboriginal girl. Where she came from I didn't know, but what I did know was that she had the most beautiful blue eyes I'd ever seen. And that, combined with her honey-coloured skin tone was a remarkable and elusive revelation.

Instantly, and despite my advanced stage of drunkenness, I was in love. The girl was high and on the nod, slurring her speech, repeatedly offering herself to me for a price.

"Wanna see a lady?"

But she wasn't any lady; she was a street kid with dirty feet, wearing a see-through blouse that revealed a pair of stiff nipples. I asked her name.

"Candice," she replied in a languid junkie drawl.

"Candice," I slurred dreamily.

Candice poked me in the shoulder. "Can you give us $50?"

"What do I get for $50?"

"Anything youse want, babes."

Anything I want? "Candice," I slurred, "I love you and want to take you away."

Candice looked at me then, her long glossy eyelashes fluttering, her body swaying towards mine, until she was in my arms.

"Where to, baby?"

"Anywhere."

12

It was a real little spontaneous community there in Barncleuth Square; almost a commune. People took it in turns to do beer runs, and food runs, and smoko runs, and generally looked out for each other. But as everyone knows, that bureaucratic wheel keeps turning, always. And so finally they showed, like a vision of doom, a clarification of reality through a subliminal alcoholic haze - the authorities. They appeared early in the morning, a couple of dead-looking council employees, grey-haired, grey suits, total millennium monochrome.

As for us, the bums, we were all hung over or beersick. I was lying on a settee, cloud viewing, and wondering if I should go a day without drinking for a change. Candice of the beautiful blue eyes, had disappeared into the remains of the night, gone forever. I knew she would and I knew I'd never see her again.

There was a half-finished bottle of gut-rot port by my side. I grabbed the bottle, figured I'd give up drinking in February, and took a hit. I scrunched up my eyes, it was filth, but afterwards I felt a little better. Beermatt was asleep on an armchair opposite, a beatific smile on his booze- and sun-red face. The two drunk women had disappeared, but lying on a rug below him was Queensland Suzie slouched in the recovery position, looking more dead than alive.

The Suits had papers, official documents, pages and pages of bureaucratic nonsense composed by imbecilic automatons. They waved those useless documents in the bloated and beer-soaked faces of the two Famous Bums, Growler and Baldie. They were asleep on a mattress, locked in each others arms like the last of God's maddened lovers. It appeared the authorities somehow knew they were the ringleaders, the creators of the Great Room. I listened in.

"We don't want any trouble," said one of the Suits. "But we are here to inform you that you must vacate the environs of Barncleuth Square within 24hrs, or face arrest and imprisonment."

Despite their serious nature, the threats sounded strangely impotent. I pulled out my battered notepad and made some quick observational sketches of the government lackeys – unremarkable individuals – well-fed, badly dressed, yet guilty of the crime of not living, just existing – all in all, a couple of walking, talking stiffs.

Growler was the first to react. "Urgggggggggggggggggggggggggggggghhhhhhhhh," he roared in his own, inimitable style.

The Suits nearly jumped out of their skins.

"I beg your pardon," said the least shaken of the two.

Next it was Baldie. He picked up an empty bottle of vino and lobbed it in the direction of the men. To be fair, it was a bit of a feeble throw as Baldie was slightly off balance, but it landed in front of the suits, exploding into a thousand fragments on impact with the pavement. Baldie smiled a toothless smile.

"Now, go on, fack off, before youse get killed!"

One of the Suits pointed an angry finger. "Now, now, we'll have none of that sort of behaviour. This Square is for everyone's enjoyment, families, children, not anti-social louts and ne'er-do-wells."

Baldie was incredulous. "Youse, ya useless piece of shit, ya ave tha audacity to come into my home and start shouting the odds. Well I'll be…"

Now it was the turn of the Suit to look incredulous. "Your home…' he stuttered.

Baldie stood up and fronted the Suit, roaring and spitting, standing to the uppermost of his tall six-foot plus frame.

"GET OUT OF MY HOUSE BEFORE I CALL THE FUCKING POLICE!" he shrieked.

The Suit backed off, quickly.

At this point Beermatt awoke from his self-imposed coma and had the awareness of mind to say something that fitted the scene.

"Unless, of course, you want to run along to the nearest bottle-shop and get the booze in amigos," he croaked.

A few of the bums cheered, and I smiled wryly.

In the meanwhile, one of the Suits began frantically writing down something on a clipboard. This was a mistake. When the Growler saw what he was up to he marched over, growling all the way. Then he poked the man in the chest, grabbed the clipboard, and Frisbee'd it into some nearby bushes. The Suit was aghast.

"You can't do that, that's g-g-g-government property," he stammered, his fat potato face blushing bright scarlet until I thought he was going to have a coronary. The Growler did what he was best at and growled some more.

"Urghhhhhhhhhhhhhhhhhhhhhhhhhhhhhh."

By now most of the other bums had been woken by the commotion, even Queensland Suzie, who much to my relief was still alive. The assorted hobos and hangers-on began jeering at the Suits. Somebody threw a bottle. Baldie and the Growler sat back in their chairs and stuck their thumbs to their noses and wiggled their fingers. It was hilarious. We all sniggered, we all cried with laughter, except the council automatons. They became strangely emboldened and began issuing threats.

"Now listen to us, this anti-social behaviour is totally unacceptable and will not be allowed to continue. This uncooperative attitude is only going to delay the inevitable," one of them shouted out from some way away.

More bottles were thrown, and a banana, even a box of old fried chicken. The Suits backed further away.

"Now we'll have none of that. Littering is a criminal offence. We're going to call the police. You'll regret this, you lot."

"Fuck off," said five or six of us in unison.

The Suits shot us one final look of disgust before turning around and disappearing round a corner.

Everyone cheered and shouted. We were now comrades in arms, unified against a common enemy, the enemies of freedom and liberty - the corrupt, morally bankrupt, and incompetent Powers That Be. It promised to be a fight to the death.

When everyone had stopped cheering and we were wondering what to do next, Beermatt called for hush. Then he eyeballed everyone.

"Right, it looks like we've got a fight on our hands to keep this here room, lovingly constructed by Baldie and Growler, open, and I figure there's only one thing to do."

"What's that?" answered the bums.

"Get fucking roaring fucking blind drunk!"

The assorted bums and hobos and freaks, cheered and shouted, until Beermatt once more called for hush. But this time there was a sparkle in his blue eyes.

"And guess what?" he whispered, mysteriously.

"What?" said the crowd.

And it was then that Beermatt did a good impression of the Milky Bar Kid.

"The drinks are on me!"

Moments later, me and Beermatt found ourselves walking to the nearest bottle-shop.

On the way we discussed the situation in hand.

"Things are getting serious," said Beermatt.

"What d'ya reckon will happen?" said I.

Beermatt appeared thoughtful. "It's a no-win situation, but from here on in its ganna be mother-fucking interesting."

At the bottle-shop, Beermatt opened the door and ushered me inside.

"Yeah, you're right," I said. "But if things gets messy, we might end up getting arrested and deported."

Beermatt began picking up bottles of the bums' favourite tipple, dirt cheap, but ultra-strong gut-rot port wine.

"That's why we don't get too involved, play a purely spectator role, then write some pomes about the event. It seems the poetic thing to do."

"It seems like the cop-out thing to do."

Beermatt shot me an incredulous look. "So you fancy a few weeks in Villawood detention centre, a one-way ticket to the UK, and a five grand deportation bond?"

I had to admit I didn't fancy any of that shit. Then I remembered my epiphany and the great Australian novel I was yet to write. Fuck it, there was no way I was getting deported. I had five years of wandering the lucky country to complete.

"Yeah, I think you're right," I mumbled, as I picked up a crate of Toohey's Red.

Beermatt smiled and patted me on the back. "Of course I'm right, now let's go."

That night another great party went down in Barncleuth Square. Everyone was there. A couple of buskers from the Blue Mountains materialised from out of nowhere, fantastic harmonica players, who got everyone in the mood with some energetic and frenetic playing. Around midnight, me, Beermatt and Queensland Suzie did a mad drunken jig, while the harmonicas blasted, and a big silver moon bathed the Square in ghostly shadows. It seemed that none of us had a care in the world, especially as the drinks kept coming; a never-ending supply of booze paid for mostly by Beermatt.

At three the party had died down a little, with quite a few bums and freaks already crashed out on various mattresses and items of furniture. Beermatt had grown maudlin.

"It's all shit, Ridgwell. Proper 100% unadulterated solidified shit."

"What is," I slurred.

Beermatt appeared misty-eyed. "Take a look around, amigo. See all these poor people, our little hobo friends and alkis? All they want to do is get pissed in the sanctuary of their own home. Is that too much to ask for?" he blubbed.

I started to feel a bit sentimental myself. "Well, I don't think it is, but the normal people, the law-abiding citizens seem to think otherwise. The odds are stacked against everyone here."

"You're dead right," said Beermatt with a suddenly demented-looking visage. "Those authority fuckers are clinical and relentless. They have taxpayers to think about, the cunts who pay their parasitical wages. All in all, they're a repressed bunch of enslaved pricks."

I felt my eyes begin to well up; I just couldn't help myself. "But what's ganna happen to all these people? To Baldie and Growler, Suzie, even the Radioman?" I bawled.

Beermatt punched a fist into an open hand. "I'm not sure, but I'm certain of one thing. They won't be going without a fight."

13

The next day the authorities arrived early, at the crack of dawn, and in numbers. It was an intimidating and somewhat depressing sight. There were nine or ten Suits, and an assortment of contractors, mostly street cleaners and bin men. I awoke on an outdoor settee with Queensland Suzie by my side. All the other bums were asleep.

One of the Suits began speaking through a megaphone. It was the same guy from the day before.

"With the power invested in us"……….etc, etc, or something like that.

I found a bottle of port wine from the previous night's drinking and took a hit. The authorities were still waffling. Then the Growler roused. He spotted the Suit and rushed over, growling all the way. He stopped inches away from the Suits face.

"Urghhhhhhhhhhhhhhhhhhhhhhhhhhhhhhhhhhhhhhhhhhhhhhh!" he roared, furiously.

The Suit backed off and surrounded himself with other Suits. I could hear him radioing for police assistance. Then the rubbish men were instructed to move in. By now Beermatt was awake, along with Queensland Suzie, and a few others.

"Oh, oh, now there'll be troubles," said Suzie.

Beermatt eyeballed the Suits and contractors. "Shit," was all he said.

"What we ganna do?" I said.

Beermatt scratched his head and rubbed his eyes. "Let's get the fuck outta here."

He grabbed my arm and we slipped quietly off into the background.

Suddenly all the bums were awake and a stand-off situation developed. Surprisingly, not one of them was prepared to back down in the face of such an organised confrontation. Growler and Baldie, with the help of some other bums, began constructing a wall of barricades.

The contractors backed off, warily and slowly. Once the barricades were up, some bottles and beer cans were thrown. By now a sizable crowd had gathered, shift workers, commuters, and early birds. The crowd watched with a mixture of revulsion and fascination. Then we heard them, the sirens.

Moments later the police arrived in numbers - six patrol cars, four vans, even a couple of motorbikes. Then we heard another noise, a distant whirring sound high above. Beermatt looked up to the sky.

"Oh for fucksakes. The cunts have only sent in a 'copter."

I looked up. Sure enough, there it was, high above, flying around in small circles, a police helicopter.

I jotted down some descriptions of the persecution in my notepad. The bums didn't stand a chance, but for a couple of hours the authorities didn't appear to know how to deal with the situation. They didn't appear to have a plan. Maybe they just thought the bums would disperse of their own accord. Fat chance, fat fucking chance. Didn't they know that Baldie and Growler were prepared to fight to the death?

The Suits kept asking the bums to vacate the Square, repeating the same tired and ineffective lines over and over through the megaphone. Each request received a volley of abuse and a barrage of whatever the bums could get their hands on - bottles, cans, bricks, even a piss-stained mattress. Cheers emanated from the crowds gathered. Fires were lit and maintained. The authorities were closing in, but just before the entire area was sealed off, me and Beermatt did a final beer run. Somehow we managed to get the grog through, a small victory in a doomed scenario.

The stand-off went on late into the night, without much happening, until just after midnight when riot police suddenly appeared on the scene. The police ordered all the bystanders to disperse, and the Square was rapidly cleared of all but the most hardcore of bums. Then they formed rows, ten men wide and four men deep, and surrounded the Great Room. The scene was like something out of the battle of the Little Bighorn and Custer's Last Stand. The bums were surrounded on all sides, and drunk and exhausted, didn't stand a chance. Me and Beermatt became totally engrossed in the scene, like we were watching a real life disaster movie.

"This is it," hissed Beermatt, wide-eyed.

I nodded, without averting my gaze from all the action.

As the net tightened the Growler eyeballed the riot police and then charged, growling all the way. "Urghhhhhhhhhhhhhhhhhhhhhhhhhhhhhhh!"

The front row of riot police was sent flying like nine pins after a perfect strike, but was replaced instantly. The Growler disappeared under an avalanche of blue uniforms. It took ten coppers to drag him away. Then the roar went up. It was party time.

A barrage of bottles and bricks and cans were hurled in the direction of the pigs, bouncing off their riot shields, until they in turn charged. Two or three ambulances were in attendance. Paramedics appeared on the scene. Police and bums were taken away on stretchers, suffering from an assortment of wounds and injuries. C.S canisters were let off and stinging smoke filled the air. Then the police charged again. The bums were sent flying, on the receiving end of batons and boots. Brutality was everywhere.

I saw Queensland Suzie and the Radioman disappear into the back of a police van; Bibi the Brazilian Trannie was taken away screaming and cussing like a banshee. Amazingly, one bum slept through the whole thing. Then, moment's later, aside from the odd disembodied shriek and desolate cry, the Battle of Barncleuth Square was over.

The next morning me and Beermatt awoke in his beat apartment, beer sick and devastated. As soon as we were able to rouse ourselves, we took a walk to Barncleuth Square. It was like none of the events had ever taken place. The authorities had been efficient in the clean-up, and only a vague memory of the Great Room remained. There wasn't a single bum in sight, or anybody for that matter. Maybe we'd imagined it all.

Beermatt turned to me. "Fuck it, I'm leaving."

I turned to Beermatt. "Leaving?"

Beermatt dug his hand into his pocket and pulled out a crumpled flight ticket. "Leaving the fucking country. I've blown the $2000, and have just enough money to get home. What are you doing?"

I stood there dumbstruck. What was I doing? Fuck knows. "Not sure, what about the flat?"

Beermatt began walking away. "You're welcome to stay there, but I've run the rent down. Only a matter of time before the agents turn up. Don't forget me."

And with that he was gone, up and away down the road, before disappearing around a corner. I stood there in Barncleuth Square not knowing what to do, and then like a miracle, I saw him. It was Baldie.

Amazingly, he had somehow avoided arrest and was capable of one final insane protest. Stark naked and covered from head to toe in fluorescent red paint, he stood there with his arms outstretched, looking like some crazed crimson Jesus Christ. As if to say,

"LOOK AT ME, LOOK WHAT YOU'VE DONE!"

And then he was gone, leaving the Cross forever, and disappearing like a red apparition into the long lost, forgotten Australian void.

Postscript I

I'm told the Cross is a sterile and somewhat soulless place these days. Spotless sidewalks and corporate coffee shops dominating an increasingly gentrified and antiseptic scene. But even though the Famous Bums are long gone and I am long gone, I'm certain of one thing. If you stand on the corner of Kellett Street and look very carefully in the direction of Barncleuth Square, you may, if lucky, see a group of spectral men and women drinking from ghostly bottles, dancing in the moonlight, and singing songs of freedom forever more.

Postscript II

Beermatt: Last known whereabouts, Africa. Last reported sighting, a bar in Mombassa drinking gin.

The Umbrella Man: Tortured, set alight, and left for dead in Rushcutters Park by two young misfits - products of a warped society that encourages human beings to commit such terrible acts of violence upon each other. For if you are brutalised then you will in turn brutalise others.

The Radioman: Whereabouts Unknown

Bibi the Brazilian Trannie: Found dead in Rat Alley in 2004. Died in suspicious circumstances, although the official cause of death was multiple organ failure brought on by years of heavy substance abuse.

The Air-Guitar Man: Last reported sighting, in the Redfern area.

Candice: Got clean, got off the game, and relocated to Brisbane. Now happily married to an Insurance salesman and has three kids.

The Instamatic Camera Lady: Passed away, 2000, aged 96 years of age.

The Growler: No reported sightings since his arrest during the Battle of Barncleuth Square. Presumed dead.

Baldie: Not seen since his final red protest.

Queensland Suzie: Found dead in the dry El Alamein fountain, just off the main drag of Darlinghurst, Kings Cross, Sydney 2001. She was 44. Some say she died of a broken heart.

Ridgwell: His plans to write the Great Australian novel never materialised and he left Australia in the year 2000. Last reported sighting, eating a burrito deluxe and drinking beer at the beach of the dead, Oaxaca, Mexico.

ABOUT US

beatthedust press

NAME: Steve Finbow
PCF NO: 8X2486359 D41577
DOB: Earlier than you think.
SEX: Never known to say no.

ALIAS: Professor Big Nose. Bug.
LAST KNOWN ADDRESS: Kumiya Bar, Tokyo.
PLACE OF BIRTH: London – The Great Wen.
RACE: What you got?

CRIMINAL CASE HISTORY

OFFENCE: Theft with Menace.
DESCRIPTION: Stealing pocket money to buy Ben Shermans. So successful, he eventually bought a velvet-collared Crombie.
DATE: 03/03/71
DISCIPLINARY ACTION: Had to write 1,000 lines on why he should not steal money from badly dressed school children.

OFFENCE: Theft.
DESCRIPTION: Stole from employer to buy books by Kerouac, Burroughs, Ginsberg, Bukowski, Celine, and Ballard.
DATE: 07/07/77
DISCIPLINARY ACTION: Sacked. 100 hours community service in a converted theatre. Spent most of the time in the pub reading above authors.

OFFENCE: Grievous Bodily Harm.
DESCRIPTION: Geezer had it coming.
DATE: 22/11/79
DISCIPLINARY ACTION: None.

OFFENCE: Serial Killer.
DESCRIPTION: Mass murderer of relationships across the world. The first offence occurred after 32 years and followed numerous botched attempts; second offence 10 years later, and the third 6 years after that. Police fear the escalation will result in numerous marriages on the same day, maybe with cult connections.
DATES: 12/09/93, 13/07/03, 31/03/09.
DISCIPLINARY ACTION: Severe financial penalties.

OFFENCE: Drug Abuse.
DESCRIPTION: Since the age of 12, continuous drug abuse including: alcohol, marijuana, cannabis, amyl nitrate, barbiturates, amphetamine sulphate, speed, LSD, cocaine, morphine, opium, heroin, and sundry other narcotics of dubious chemistry. Current drugs include: ramipril, bendroflumethiazide, simvastin, amlodipine, doxazosin mesilate, novorapid, insulin glargine, and

Stella Artois.

DATE: Circa 1973-present.

DISCIPLINARY ACTION: Blackouts, kidney failure, pancreatitis, and four different types of coma.

OFFENCE: Mind Theft.

DESCRIPTION: Charged with lifting ideas and lines from other writers.

DATE: Unknown.

DISCIPLINARY ACTION: Unproven but he can feel the heat closing in.

NAME: Melissa Mann
PCF NO: 6X1300318 D31389
DOB: Unknown. S'a mystery.
RACE: 400 metres hurdles.

ALIAS: Morrissey with tits. And balls.
LAST KNOWN ADDRESS: Walthamstow, East London.
PLACE OF BIRTH: Bradford, Capital of England.
SEX: Never. Saving herself for Russell Brand.

CRIMINAL CASE HISTORY

OFFENCE: Burglary and Attempted Arson
DESCRIPTION: Detained in the act of setting fire to a classroom using a magnifying glass stolen from the science labs, and a copy of *The History of Mr Polly*.
DATE: 03/07/83
DISCIPLINARY ACTION: Ten lashes with a black slip-on gym shoe, size 2, and a custodial sentence of two weeks' detention.

OFFENCE: Abandonment
DESCRIPTION: Renunciation of a career in management consultancy in favour of a more fulfilling life spent writing and teaching Pilates to the inflexible and infirm of London.
DATE: 14/04/05
DISCIPLINARY ACTION: Fined £175,000. Court considered eight years shackled to a desk in the City to be a sufficient custodial sentence. Defendant was deemed to have served her time.

OFFENCE: Indecent Exposure
DESCRIPTION: Accused of exposing, in an open and obscene manner, the private parts of herself in stories and poems published widely in print magazines, anthologies and online.
DATE: 21/05/07
DISCIPLINARY ACTION: Acquitted. Court ruled that the defendant did not write with intent to cause alarm or offend others.

OFFENCE: Terrorism
DESCRIPTION: Detained under the Terrorism Act for her leadership role in the fundamentalist literary group, Beat the Dust. Accused of the systematic use of free radical poetry and prose from underground writers across the globe, to coerce and create fear within the mainstream literary world.
DATE: 15/10/07
DISCIPLINARY ACTION: Case dismissed. Court ruled the action brought against the accused by Richard & Judy, was a clear attempt by them to delegitimise a worthy opponent.

OFFENCE: Public Disorder
DESCRIPTION: Accused of hijacking the stage at a prestigious arts festival on the South Bank, London, and attempting to read a story that caused the middle-class families present to fear for their safety.
DATE: 25/05/2009
DISCIPLINARY ACTION: Released without charge. The court agreed with the defendant that the event was a poorly organized, pretentious pile of doggy-doo-doo that needed shaking up.

OFFENCE: Unlawful Trading
DESCRIPTION: Charged under the Mainstream Poetry Act for trading without a Poetic licence. 150 copies of her debut collection *baby, i'm ready to go* were seized by the court.
DATE: 31/08/2009
DISCIPLINARY ACTION: Found guilty. Given 90 days community work reading the complete works of Byron and Shelley to secondary school kids with special needs in the London Borough of Hackney.

NAME: Joseph Ridgwell
PCF NO: 5Q2477490 C53372

DOB: 1970s
RACE: English, Irish, French, Spanish

ALIAS: Literary thug boozer.
LAST KNOWN ADDRESS: Kellett St, Kings Cross, Sydney, NSW 2011, Australia.
PLACE OF BIRTH: East London.
SEX: Strictly threesomes.

BEST KNOWN APHORISMS: 'If you join them, you will always be at odds with them, and everything they stand for.'

CRIMINAL CASE HISTORY

OFFENCE: The Search for the Lost Elation
DESCRIPTION: Has smoked it, drunk it, stabbed it, fucked it, written about it, and if he put it all down here, they'd just lift him again for it…